Into the Golden Dawn

RASPBERRY RIDGE
BOOK FIVE

JESSIE GUSSMAN

Contents

Acknowledgments

Cover art by Julia Gussman
Editing by Heather Hayden
Narration by Jay Dyess
Author Services by CE Author Assistant

Listen to the unabridged audio for FREE performed by Jay Dyess on the Say with Jay channel on YouTube. Get early access to all of Jay's recordings and listen to Jessie's books before they're available to the general public, plus get daily Bible readings by Jay and bonus scenes by becoming a Say with Jay channel member.

One

This was not the time or place.

Olive Jardine stared at the man walking toward her, knowing she had a lot of explaining to do, and even more apologizing, but she stood at the back of the church in the middle of a church service, although it was well after noon on Sunday in Raspberry Ridge, Michigan. The town she'd grown up in. The town she'd spent her childhood in, although her parents had moved away before she graduated from high school.

Doyle McKenny, the man who had almost reached her side, was part of the reason she hadn't been back in years.

"Olive? Is that you?"

Olive swallowed hard. There was amazement on his face, but there was also a hint of the hurt that she'd inflicted, and once he knew for sure that it was her, she was sure that part of his expression would balloon into something she could hardly stand. Perhaps there would also be hate.

She glanced around the church. A couple of heads had turned when Doyle got up, but Olive's sister, Mertie, and some man Olive was pretty sure was Mertie's best friend from childhood, stood in front of the microphone, speaking, and most people were hanging on their every word.

Olive hadn't taken the time to try to figure out what they were saying. She'd been too shocked when she'd stepped in and seen the back of Doyle's head. It was unmistakable, since he was taller than everyone in the sanctuary, and if that wasn't enough to set him apart, he had hair the color of carrots.

Back in their childhood, when she had described his hair that way, he had always laughed. It hadn't bothered him a bit, even though originally Olive had said it as an insult, since Anne, from Anne of Green Gables, had been so upset about the comparison.

Men were different. At least Doyle was different.

She hadn't realized how different, maybe special was a better word, until she had travelled the world a little. It hadn't taken her long to realize that what she had left behind in Raspberry Ridge, thinking that there was something better out there, had been the best.

It amazed her sometimes that God had started her out with the very best.

It also frustrated her that she hadn't been smarter, more aware, more grateful.

"Olive?" Doyle said again, and she realized she hadn't answered him.

"Not now," she said, more because she didn't know what to say than because she couldn't have told him she wanted to go outside and talk.

She met his eyes again, deep, deep green, and felt the inexpressible shiver that went up and down her spine.

His eyes narrowed, but his gaze didn't move away.

She allowed her eyes to linger for just another moment, noting the square jaw, the sharp nose, the laugh lines at the corners of his mouth and eyes that didn't used to be there, before she turned, hooking her arm in the handle of the car seat and straightening back up.

Her eyes shifted back to his once more, even though she didn't mean for them to, and she caught the surprise, betrayal, the...hurt. She had hurt this good man, badly, and yet he had come to her, not with anger, but with curiosity, and...maybe even forgiveness?

But now, seeing the baby she held, the open expression in his eyes closed, and his gaze became guarded.

"Yours?" he said, low, under the murmur of the people speaking at the front of the church.

She nodded. Ashamed, but keeping her chin up. She'd made mistakes, a lot of them, but she didn't regret her daughter. Maybe she regretted the circumstances, regretted the decisions that led her to Ecuador and all of the things that happened there, but she could never regret her little girl.

Doyle nodded curtly, then, rather than turning and going back to his seat, he murmured, "Excuse me," and then walked around her and went silently out the back door.

She wanted to follow him, wanted to explain, to beg forgiveness, to make things right between them, but she wasn't sure that was possible.

Finding an open pew toward the back, she set her baby down, who was thankfully still sleeping, and slipped in beside her.

Livvy was a good baby, which was one of the many blessings that at one point in her life she might not have been thankful for, but she was so grateful for now. God had been so good to her, and she hadn't appreciated much of anything.

When she had been lying in her hospital bed in Ecuador, not sure whether she was going to live or die, barely conscious, and having no clue of who was watching her child, she had promised herself that if she got out of this, she would make a point to be grateful to God every day, for the many things that He did for her that she, up until that point, had taken for granted.

Things like waking up with no pain, being able to breathe without thinking about it, growing up in a small town in a country like the United States, which, while it was not perfect, was better than any other country she'd ever visited.

Better because of the freedom, better because of the open friendliness of the people, better because of the godly heritage she didn't even realize she rested on.

She hadn't been taught to stop and appreciate things. She'd been taught to constantly strive for more, like what she had wasn't enough, when it certainly was.

Although, right now it wasn't. But she'd cross that bridge later.

"I wanted to give everyone a chance to ask any questions they wanted to. So, we'll open the floor up for that right now."

The man at the front, who looked so much like Garnet, her sister Mertie's longtime childhood friend, that Olive couldn't believe it would be anyone else, stood at the microphone, one arm around Mertie and one around some young girl that looked like a carbon copy of Mertie beside him.

"I didn't think you were married. But your daughter looks exactly like Mertie Jardine. What's going on?"

From where she sat in the back, Olive couldn't tell who was speaking. It had been years since she had been back to Raspberry Ridge, and while she almost certainly knew the person, people changed, and looking at the backs of their heads didn't give her much of a hint.

But the question struck her, because the man was right. The little girl that stood beside her sister looked exactly like her sister, but as far as she knew, Mertie didn't have any children.

"Well, that's a good question." Garnet spoke, glancing at Mertie, who gave a small nod, before glancing at the young girl, who nodded as well. The girl shifted, slipping her arm through Mertie's, and Mertie reached over with her other hand, patting the girl's fingers and then holding them.

It was a sign of comfort and solidarity, and it made Olive smile to see it.

"Mertie and I are planning on getting married. I didn't mention this when I was candidating, but since the Bible clearly says that a pastor should be the husband of one wife, I wasn't going to accept the pastorate on a full-time basis if I wasn't married. That was just something between the Lord and me, something I knew needed to happen in order for me to be a pastor."

There were a few murmurs in the congregation, but most people seemed to be accepting.

"Mertie and I have decided to get married, and I've already spoken with Dominic, the head deacon. He has agreed that I won't be on full-time until Mertie and I have set a date and are actually married in the sight of God. We don't know when that's going to be, but soon." He glanced over at Mertie, and she gave him such a soft, sweet smile, so uncharacteristic of her commanding, in-charge, always-plowing-ahead older sister, that it almost made Olive tear up.

Would she ever give such a tender look to a man?

She glanced down at Livvy, sleeping quietly beside her. There had been no tender looks, nothing with the kind of love in it that flowed between Mertie and Garnet. Of course, Mertie and Garnet had always been friends, good friends, and now, with her travels under her belt, Olive thought that perhaps being friends was a prerequisite to being more.

She couldn't imagine getting married to someone she didn't like. Lust and like were two different things. She wished she hadn't needed to travel to Ecuador to find that out.

She wouldn't have minded if she had never found that out, and she wouldn't have, if she had taken what God had put right in front of her. Doyle.

"What about your daughter? Dabney?" the man reiterated.

"There are some things that we need to discuss among the three of us before I can answer the rest of that question. I know you understand. I'm not trying to hide anything, I just can't give some information out before certain things have been taken care of."

The man nodded, and then someone else said, "We might not have hired you if we had known you'd had a child out of wedlock."

"And that's reasonable," Garnet said, not seeming to be angered by the statement at all. "I feel like I would have been misleading you if I had not told you that I had a child out of wedlock. But I did not. I adopted Dabney when she was a baby, but I had nothing to do with her conception."

"You and Mertie were good friends. And that looks like Mertie's daughter."

Olive had come to the same conclusion, and after glancing around the congregation to see who had spoken, she looked back toward Garnet to see what he would say.

"We were good friends. We are good friends. And she does look a lot like Mertie. I promise, we will tell you everything, but there are a few other things that we need to do before we can do that." He lifted his brows. "Any other questions?"

"Are you going to go to the hospitals and do visits? Visit nursing homes? Work with us to figure out how we might be able to grow our congregation?"

Garnet started to answer, and Olive tried to pay attention, but her mind wandered, wondering where Doyle had gone and feeling bad that he had left what was obviously an important meeting for the Raspberry Ridge congregation.

The meeting dragged on, and Livvy started to stir.

She stood up, grabbing the handle to slip back out of the church, when her eyes met the eyes of a woman who had turned around. She was sitting beside a man, his arm around her shoulders, and he looked down at her as she turned.

Amara. Her sister. She recognized her almost immediately. And just after she did, Amara's eyes lit up with recognition, and she hopped a little in her seat, then turned quickly to the man beside her and whispered furiously in his ear before she stood up, walked in front of him out the end of the pew, and hurried back to Olive.

"Olive!" she said softly, but her voice burst with excitement. "You're here!" She went to throw her arms around Olive, but just at the last second, she saw the car seat Olive held.

Olive hadn't mentioned the pregnancy, hadn't mentioned the ill-fated relationship, hadn't mentioned all of her regrets, and had not mentioned Livvy.

In fact, the excuses that she had given for not coming to Raspberry Ridge sooner had been just that, excuses, most of which had not been true, which Olive hated. But she hadn't wanted her sisters to worry. If they had known that she was lying in an Ecuadorian hospital, near death, they might have tried to find a way to get down to her, and she knew that neither one of her sisters, with their high-paying jobs, would have time to do that.

"Let's go outside," she said softly, wondering if she could put Amara off until Mertie was with them. That way, she wouldn't have to tell the story twice.

But it looked like she was going to have to tell it to the men in her sisters' lives as well as her sisters, since both of them seemed to have gotten attached to someone since the last time Olive had seen them.

Amara nodded, some of the excitement slipping off her face and concern and confusion replacing it. But she waited while Olive squeezed out of the pew, which was thankfully still empty, and carried the car seat with an awakening baby Livvy in it to the back, slipping out and into the bright Michigan sunlight.

The lake shone, deep blue and sparkling in the distance. She always loved this view. As she took a moment to stare at it now, taking in a deep breath and letting it ground her, center her, it fixed her thoughts on what was important. God. Bringing glory to Him. Bringing others to Him. It wasn't about her. Whatever her sisters' reactions were to what she had done, she couldn't control them and didn't need to be worried or upset about them. She could regret her actions while admitting that she had determined not to do them again.

That she had changed.

"Whose baby is this?" Amara asked, as soon as the door clicked closed behind them.

"Mine." She knew that was going to open a whole plethora of more questions, but she still hoped to head them off.

"When did you have a baby? I didn't even know you were pregnant!" Amara looked at her in amazement. "It wasn't that long ago that we cleaned out the condo in Chicago. You weren't pregnant then."

"It was winter. I wore bulky shirts. Sweatshirts. Coats. You guys just didn't notice, and I wasn't showing that much."

"I guess I remember that. I remember thinking you'd put on a little weight, but I hadn't realized that it wasn't just a little weight."

"It's legit that you have questions, but if you don't mind, I'm going to assume that Mertie has the same questions."

"I wondered if she knew things I didn't, and she just wasn't telling me!"

"No. I haven't told either of you. There's...a lot we need to catch up on."

"Well, this afternoon seems like a good time to do it, although Mertie might be tired. It's a big day for her."

"What was going on?" She had assumed that Garnet had been sworn in as pastor, but why was Mertie up there with him?

"Today the church voted Garnet in as pastor."

"What was Mertie doing up there with him?" she asked as they walked down the steps and away from the door a little bit. She didn't think their voices would carry into the sanctuary, but just in case, it was better to be safe than sorry. Plus, she needed to get a bottle out of her bag since Livvy was starting to fuss.

"She and Garnet are together. At least, I think so. Everything happened so quickly."

"Then maybe we should just all have a get-caught-up session, because I noticed that you were sitting with a man I didn't recognize."

"Yeah, we'll definitely need a session for that. You aren't going to believe what happened to me, and I need some time to explain, because you might be upset at first." That was actually a relief to hear, that she wasn't the only one with news that might be upsetting to her siblings.

"After Mom and Dad died, I thought that we would be closer than ever. You know? I wanted that."

"I still want that! But it's hard to be close to someone who's halfway around the world."

"I'm here to stay. At least stay as long as I can get a job and support myself."

Amara stared at her, looking confused, then thoughtful.

Olive allowed the baby bag to slip off her shoulder as she set the car seat down and knelt beside it, digging in her bag for the bottle of water she kept there and the formula, grabbing both, and setting everything out to get ready to feed Livvy.

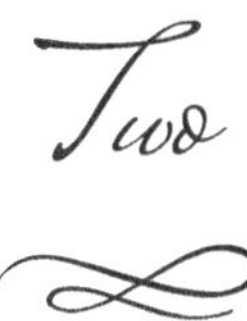

Two

"It's okay if I get her out?" Amara asked Olive, kneeling down beside Livvy.

"I would appreciate it. I've fed her in worse places, and I've often fed her without getting her out of her car seat, but she needs to be snuggled."

Especially since she hadn't gotten that after she had first been born.

As her sister unstrapped the baby and carefully got her out, she casually said, "I think there are some other things we need to talk about. You might not have gotten all the correspondence that our parents' lawyers have been sending about their estate."

"I haven't gotten a single one," Olive said, not really thinking a whole lot about it. Just hoping that she didn't have a lot of bills to pay, because she certainly couldn't afford it. Weren't lawyers expensive?

"I think she needs a diaper change," Amara said as she lifted Livvy carefully and cradled her in one arm.

"I have a little pad you can set her on, if you don't mind?"

"I don't mind at all, but I can count on one hand the number of diapers I've changed in my life. So, while I know it doesn't go on her head, I'm not sure I'm going to get it right."

"You have to start somewhere. And Livvy is as easygoing as a baby can get. She's put up with quite a few novice diaper changes from me. I'm still not great at it."

"I suppose practice makes perfect. And she doesn't look very old."

"She's not. Just two months."

"Wow. I can't believe I didn't know you were pregnant."

"I love bulky sweatshirts."

"You always have. So I didn't think anything about it when I saw you in them."

"It was great camouflage. Although, I was definitely tempted to tell you guys. I just...didn't."

She hadn't completely broken up with Ricardo at the time. And she had needed to go back to Ecuador. She didn't want her sisters trying to talk her out of it, even though at that point, she knew that it wasn't a good idea.

She wished she had talked to them and allowed them to talk her out of it. But the lessons that she learned after she'd gotten so deathly ill, after Ricardo had left her without a backward glance, after she'd suffered through the most difficult time of her life, those lessons were priceless. And they brought her back to the Lord. It was funny how when everything was going well, she hadn't given God much thought, but as soon as her life was in danger, and her daughter was potentially going to lose her mother, and she had no one else to turn to, she clung to God, and to her surprise, He answered her prayers.

He didn't seem to hold a grudge because she had basically ignored Him all her life. God was forgiving, and He proved that to her, which had made her want to do more for Him, because He had done so much for her.

It had been the hardest time of her life, but it had completely changed her life, so while she wished she had said something to her sisters, she also was glad she hadn't.

"Is this too tight?" her sister asked as she put the tabs around the baby's belly.

Livvy had started crying, although from experience, Olive knew that her cries could get a lot louder than what they were.

"I don't think so. If it's too loose, it'll fall off, but I haven't gotten it too tight yet."

It was one mistake she hadn't made. Or maybe it was one mistake she just didn't realize she had made. It was probably like a too-tight pair of jeans, it would be uncomfortable, but at least it wouldn't fall off and allow leakage to go everywhere.

"So," Amara said, studiously studying the diaper that she had just put on the baby. "Are you going to answer any of my questions?"

"I know I owe answers to you, but I owe them to Mertie too. Can we maybe wait until the three of us are together, so I can tell the story just once?"

Olive knew that her sisters deserved to know what was going on in her life. They were her sisters after all. And she hadn't been forthcoming with them. In fact, as terrible as she felt about it, she'd told lies to keep them from worrying. She was going to have to admit that too. And she definitely didn't want to.

"That makes sense. Mertie already knows my story, but you don't. Maybe I should tell you."

"I'd like to hear," she said as she picked up the supplies, smiling as Amara picked up the baby. She held her like she didn't quite know what to do with her, but it was obvious that she was also enchanted.

"She's so perfect."

"My opinion might be biased, but I agree with that assessment."

Her sister laughed. They had so many good memories together. But as they had grown older, especially after they moved away from Raspberry Ridge, there had been less and less family time and more time where she pursued her own interests. Of course she had been a teenager, but she thought of herself as selfish. Maybe she could also blame her parents. They seemed less and less interested in the fact that they had a family. And less and less interested in keeping the family together.

When Amara didn't start right away, she prompted her, "If you don't want to tell me, you don't have to."

"I was just trying to figure out where to start. There's so much baggage with our parents."

"I was just thinking it was pretty amazing that they stayed together, like, they would have been the prime candidates for divorce. I never really thought they liked each other that much."

"You know, I hadn't thought about that, but I think you're right.

They never did seem to care for each other. And they definitely didn't try to spend time with each other."

"Isn't that what normal people want?" Honestly, she wasn't even sure what normal was.

"Well, maybe that's part of my story. Since, I'm engaged to be married, and I want to spend every waking second with my fiancé."

"Someone I know?"

"And that's where my story starts," Amara said, holding her hand out for the bottle, and after a pause, Olive held it out.

"You want to go over there to the bench?" she asked, nodding at the bench that sat just outside of the cemetery, facing the lake.

"Yes. I think I would do better if I were sitting down," Amara said with a smile. "My job in Chicago didn't exactly prepare me for feeding babies."

"No. You were doing really well in that job. How soon do you have to go back? Is that where your fiancé is from? Chicago?"

"Goodness. A lot has happened in the last few weeks. When I got here, I met Hobert Gilchrest, maybe you—"

"The kid from our childhood that we weren't allowed to talk to?" Olive said in disbelief. She remembered well her mother's warnings to stay far, far away from him, that he was bad and no good. They weren't even allowed to talk to him on the school bus, let alone to play with him.

"The very one. I know Mom always told us not to talk to him, and I found out why."

"Why? Did he kill someone?"

"He was a kid. In elementary school. Of course he wasn't a murderer."

"True. But now? Is he in jail?"

"No. I'm engaged to him."

"Shut up." Olive said in disbelief. There was no way her sister could be getting married to the notorious Hobert Gilchrest. There had to be a catch. She had to be joking.

"Yes. When I first met him, I didn't know who he was and he didn't know who I was. I think we both suspected each other's identities, but I got to the point where I really didn't want to know. Because I found out he was actually a really great guy. Humble, kind, and hardworking, and he had his head on straight. You know? Where I had a tendency to get caught up in my work and get lost in it, and maybe even neglect the things that I shouldn't, like you."

She looked over. "I didn't even know my own sister was pregnant. You think I might have been working too much?" She laughed, but it lacked a lot of humor. "Anyway, when I found out his name, I had to try to dig around and figure out why Mom always told us he was no good. It turns out Mertie found her journals, and we found out that it had to do with the fact that the husband of one of Mom's friends had an affair with Hobert's mother. So basically, Mom was angry, her friend was hurt and lost her marriage, and it was a mess. But Hobert was an innocent bystander who happened to be the one that Mom took her anger out on."

"A child? She would honestly punish a child because of what his parents did?"

"It looks that way. According to her journal. I assume she wasn't lying in them."

"No. That's probably the one place where you tell the truth."

She hadn't realized her mom had journals, although now that she thought about it, she supposed she'd seen her mom writing at various times in little notebooks. She supposed she just thought that she was figuring out a new sales plan or something.

"So, Hobert and I are getting married, and we're going to build a house down by where his house is now. Something a little bit bigger than what he has, but nothing ostentatious or massive. I... I learned a lot from Hobert and his idea of living simply, not getting a bunch of stuff you don't need, and not working so hard that you never really get to enjoy the fruits of your labor, and it all kind of rubbed off on me and... I quit my job in Chicago."

"What?" Olive said, pausing as they reached the bench.

Livvy had really started to cry, and maybe she had misheard her sister.

"I quit my job." Her words were simple, then she looked back down at the baby and sat carefully, bringing the bottle up and touching her lips with it before Livvy figured out what was going on and latched onto the nipple immediately.

"I can't believe it." Which was absolutely true. Her sister had been so determined to climb the ladder and reach the top, becoming the first whatever it was that she was, which Olive wasn't even sure. Just knew it was a bigwig thing in Chicago, and Amara was living the Chicago life and seemed to enjoy it.

"So you had a radical transformation." It wasn't a question, but she still tilted her head and watched Amara's reaction.

"I did. I guess I always knew that wasn't the right way to live. That I loved my small town, and I was much happier here, but I got sucked into wanting more and being better and all that, and I guess that just became what I thought I wanted. But it's not anymore."

"And you said that you and Hobert are engaged?"

"Yes. We don't want a big fancy wedding. We just want something small, as soon as Garnet...Pastor Garnet I guess he is now, can marry us."

"So that was Garnet. Mertie's best friend from childhood?"

"Yes. There's...something going on with them. I know they're getting married, but it was so shocking. Mertie told me that she owed me an explanation, so maybe it's good that we'll plan to get together, and everybody can tell everyone else their stories. Except everyone knows mine now."

"Yours is pretty amazing, and you have a happily ever after."

"I don't know if I would go that far. There's going to be a lot of life to live between now and the time it's over. Hopefully anyway. Who knows what God has for us."

"Yeah. Sometimes God has really wonderful things for us and we just turn our heads and walk away."

"You sound like you're talking from experience."

"I might be."

Her sister looked interested, but she didn't say anything more. If she was going to wait to tell her story, there was no point in getting it started now. Instead, she smiled at the way Amara cradled Livvy, looking down on her like she was fascinating.

Until she had become a mom, she didn't realize how much a parent might enjoy having someone make a fuss over their child. It warmed her heart every time someone said something kind about Livvy, like it was somehow like a compliment for her, only better. Not that she felt she could take any credit at all for what Livvy was—a good baby who hardly ever fussed except when she was hungry or needed to be changed. Olive certainly didn't have that kind of personality. At least she didn't used to. She was working on shifting her entire being, and having God in her life had helped that process considerably. She couldn't do it by herself.

"Where are you staying?" Amara asked, her head popping up like she had just thought about it.

"I'm not sure. I came to the church, not because I knew there was something going on, but because I wanted a place to pray. I knew that this visit was going to be difficult in a lot of different ways, and I just wanted God's blessing on it. I didn't realize I was going to be walking into..."

She wasn't sure what she had walked into.

"The congregation had just voted to have Garnet as their pastor. He was thanking them for voting for him, and then he was fielding questions."

"Wow. So when does he start?"

"I'm not sure."

That seemed to stir up more questions in Olive than it answered, but hopefully all of their concerns and questions would be answered this afternoon when the sisters got together.

In the meantime, Olive had to admit, as her eyes scanned over the wide blue expanse of the lake, it felt good to be home.

Three

Had he been dreaming?

Doyle McKenny could hardly believe that he had just seen Olive Jardine, his friend from childhood, but more than that, the woman who had taken his heart and ripped it apart, then thrown it back at his feet. He'd offered her everything he had, and it hadn't been good enough for her.

And foolishly, as he seemed to be any time Olive was around, he had run to her the first moment he'd seen her back in years, hoping that she'd finally come back to him.

Instead, she had someone else's baby at her feet.

Doyle stroked through the lake, the cold water not doing anything to cool his hurt or his anger.

The anger had surfaced slowly, dug out from years of him burying it, using every excuse in the book to try to explain away why Olive had done what she had to him.

But now, seeing her back, seeing that the excuses that she'd given him had been just that, excuses, and realizing that he'd been a fool to carry a torch for her for so long, the anger couldn't be suppressed any longer.

He swam a mile up the beach before he turned around, swimming back to the pebble beach at Raspberry Ridge. It was a nice, secluded beach, and because of the shape of the shoreline that protected it from large waves, typically there was no undertow.

It was a perfect place to take a swim. Which he usually did every morning starting about April, in his wetsuit. Since full summer had descended, the water hadn't warmed up too much, but he no longer wore the wetsuit.

Not that he would have taken the time to put it on today anyway. As shocked as he had been from seeing Olive.

Why had she come back? And why had he run to her? Why couldn't he stay away?

Those questions rolled around his mind as he swam the rest of the way back and considered turning around and tacking another two miles on the two he'd already done. He didn't feel nearly worn out enough. So frustrated with himself.

But then, from his vantage point, he could see a car moving along the cliff and figured that church had probably let out. Actually, it might be empty.

He had already spoken with the new pastor about his need for a housekeeper. He figured in a place like Raspberry Ridge, the little country store owner and the pastor were the two people who probably saw most of the population on a regular basis.

If he was going to manage his company, a property management company, from his new base at Raspberry Ridge, he wasn't going to be able to do it if he had to cook all of his own meals and clean up after himself.

The housekeeper that he'd had in Chicago had made him uncomfortable, but he'd still offered her the job in Raspberry Ridge, but she'd never gotten back to him. Which was just as well with him, since she made him uncomfortable. She was a little too...clingy? Nosy? Close. She just wanted to be too close to him.

Still, he was happy with his decision to move to Raspberry Ridge, at least he had been. Until he'd seen Olive. And her baby. And figured that there must be a husband around somewhere.

He finished walking out of the water, grabbing a small towel from where he'd left it on the beach along with his clothes. He ran it through his hair and swiped to get most of the water off his arms and torso and limbs before sticking his clothes back on.

He couldn't do this in Chicago, take a spontaneous swim whenever he felt like it. There were definitely perks to coming back, even though he'd left most of the infrastructure that made doing business in the city so nice. The chance that you'd run into someone that you could do business with, or make a deal with, or who could scratch your back while you scratched theirs was much higher in Chicago than it had been here in Raspberry Ridge, but more and more people were going to working online, and the in-person benefits were declining.

Plus, he had gotten tired of the city. It was distracting, which is what he needed after Olive had left him, but it didn't feed his soul and make him want to be a better person the way standing on the shores of Lake Michigan, looking out into the deep, wide expanse, and remembering the God who created it all did. That really made him want to step up and be better.

As he walked up on the beach, he saw Homer walking hand in hand with his wife Skyler, their young daughter tucked in one arm, as his wife held her arm around his mother, Gertie.

Gertie seemed to be in and out as the Alzheimer's that she was fighting with took over more and more of her mind, but Homer had told him that he thought exercise was good for her, and as long as she wanted to continue to take walks, he would make the time.

He had gotten a good wife, one who obviously loved him and who loved his mother as well and took excellent care of her.

Why couldn't he have fallen for someone like that?

Instead, he fell for someone who left him, saying that she just wanted to spread her wings a little and that she would come back for him, except...she hadn't.

She hadn't stayed in touch, hadn't even kept up on social media. To his chagrin, he'd checked.

Sometimes he was just so desperate for any news of her, any news at all, that he couldn't help checking her socials to see if she might be posting something, anything.

Maybe she had lied. Maybe her breakup speech was exactly that—an "I never want to see you again" type of thing.

"Hey there," Homer said as they met along the beach.

"It's a nice day for a swim," he replied, nodding at Skyler and Miss Gertie.

They nodded back and smiled, and then Miss Gertie pointed to something ahead, and Skyler walked along with her.

Homer let her go and then shifted the baby from one arm to the other.

"What do you think of the new pastor?" Homer asked, and Doyle assumed he was just making conversation.

"I liked him. His messages were straight from the Bible, and he gave chapter and verse for the things that he said. I don't want a man who's going to go up there and just shout out his opinion for an hour."

"Me either. I wouldn't have voted for someone like that, even if his opinion aligns with mine. What's the point in that? I'm not going to be challenged, I'm not going to grow as a Christian if we just have someone who has an opinion that agrees with mine."

"Right. That's why I asked the question I did, making sure that he was going to preach the Bible and not use his opinions as the basis for his sermons."

"I'm satisfied that he's not going to. I've been going to the daily Bible studies he's been doing in the morning. Actually, we started them at my house, but they've moved them to his because his parents aren't getting around well enough to come down. And it seemed kind of important that his mom be there."

"That was considerate of you. Makes it a little bit harder for you."

"Right now, my mom's getting around just as well as she always has almost. Maybe someday she won't be, and we'll cross that bridge when we come to it. In the meantime, I just appreciate the fact that there's someone leading the Bible study and so many people are coming and getting things out of it."

"What book are you studying?"

"We're actually reading through the entire Bible. That's what the study is. We read a few chapters, and Garnet gives his thoughts on them. He might apply them to our lives, show how we can use that scripture in our daily life, but for the most part, it's more teaching than preaching."

"It sounds good. Anyone can come?"

Homer smiled. "Yep. The only requirement is you have to bring food." He looked serious for a moment, then his face broke into another grin. "All right. Maybe I made that up, and to be honest, there's always more than enough food to go around. But in my opinion, a Bible study can never have too much food."

"I'm in agreement with that opinion. I'll see what I can do, although I'm looking for a housekeeper right now. I don't do a whole lot of cooking myself, and what I do is barely edible. But when a man gets hungry enough, he can eat barely edible."

"I know what you're talking about, although I've mostly always lived with my mom. So, the times I've had to eat barely edible are few and far between, and I'm pretty sure you can tell." Homer patted his stomach with the hand that wasn't holding the baby.

She was a cute little thing, with her head wrapped up in a blue bonnet and her little eyes closed.

Is Olive's baby a boy or a girl?

The thought came unbidden, and he tried to shove it away. He didn't care about her baby, didn't care about her, didn't care about the man that she married or the life she was living. Hopefully she was just here in Raspberry Ridge for a short visit and would be moving along soon. He wasn't sure if she was staying, that he could stay as well.

It was on the tip of his tongue to ask Homer about her, but he didn't want to draw attention to the fact that he was curious about her. Because he wasn't really.

He was lying to himself. He was curious. He did want to know. Anything that anyone could tell him about her, he would love to hear.

"All right, I'm going to head up. I don't want to miss my Sunday afternoon nap."

"I'm gonna get mine here as soon as the ladies have a walk. Hopefully the baby stays asleep long enough for me to take at least a short one."

"Twenty minutes is supposed to be the ideal time, although I'm not sure I've ever found that to be true."

"Twenty minutes is better than nothing," Homer said, lifting his brows like he knew what he was talking about. And with a baby to raise, he probably did.

The thought of the baby pushed Doyle's thoughts back toward Olive, but he did not allow the things that swirled in his brain to take over. He wasn't going to think about her. He had his chance, and she said no, and that was all there was to it. He had to accept that.

Four

"And that's how it happened. Even though I'd been offered that huge opportunity with another Christian speaker, an opportunity that will never come around again, I know that wasn't what God wanted for me. It was just something the devil was tempting me with. I knew it was more important for me to be a mom than a speaker, and the more I got to know Garnet, the more I knew that God was calling me to be a pastor's wife."

Olive remembered Mertie as being confident, someone who forged ahead, who always knew exactly where she was going and what she was doing and saw the world in very black-and-white terms. This new, more reflective woman sitting in front of her didn't seem like her sister at all. Except, she looked just like her.

The three sisters had gone to their parents' mansion while the men had stayed away to give them time to chat. Garnet had Dabney and was doing something with her and his mom this afternoon so that Mertie could get away.

"I can't believe you had a baby and I didn't even know it."

"I didn't realize that Garnet had her. I thought she had been adopted somewhere." Mertie shrugged her shoulders and shook her head, looking out over the tops of her sisters' heads. "That's why when I saw her, it hit me: I need to be here. I had been given a second opportunity. And of course, Garnet was just as amazing as he always had been."

"But you guys were never boyfriend and girlfriend. You were just... friends," Amara said, taking a sip of her tea.

"It's true we were friends, but I guess I did feel some kind of strange pull, which must have been attraction, even when we were younger. But that didn't fit in with my life plan, and so I ignored it."

She couldn't imagine giving a child up for adoption. That had to have been so hard. She looked at her daughter, sleeping in the car seat beside her, and thought of all she had been through to stay with her. The idea of allowing someone else to raise her was just unthinkable.

"The sacrifice you made because of your love for your daughter, making sure that she had someone who would do a good job of raising her, knowing that you couldn't, that's just...amazing."

Her sisters had grown up. And she hadn't even noticed. Of course, hopefully they would notice that she had grown up as well.

"How soon are you guys getting married?" Amara asked, giving a little sheepish smile. "I know everything is very new. But have you given any thought to a date?"

"We want to do it as soon as possible. He didn't want to take the pastorate unless he was married. He honestly didn't think God was going to open that door. But again, Garnet is sure this is what he is supposed to be doing so he wants to get settled as soon as we can. But I need to talk to Dabney. I've chatted with her a bit, and she seemed excited to have a mom, but I know I need to have a deeper conversation. Explain exactly what was going on, why I did what I did, apologize, I don't know. I've been praying hard about it, that whenever we talk, I'll just say the things I need to say, and that God will open her heart and mind and let her forgive me."

"She should appreciate you. That's a huge sacrifice to give up your baby. I was just sitting here trying to figure out if I could, and I don't think I could."

"There was a very selfish part of me that thought that was the best thing for everyone and didn't really want to take the time to raise a baby. I would be lying if I didn't say that, but I don't think that's probably something I'm going to say a whole lot about, or at least dwell on, with Dabney. She deserves the truth, but I want her to know, I want to emphasize the fact that I loved her."

"That's what's really important. I believe that if you had thought it would be best for you to keep her, you would have given up your career for it." Amara always seemed to see the best in people. Olive was a little jealous over it. She was the one who was never bothered by much of anything, but she did notice people's flaws, and sometimes they grew huge in her eyes when she really shouldn't allow them to.

"I hope so. I guess we'll never know for sure, but that's what I want to think. That I would have chosen the better way, even though I was young and sometimes when we're young, we just make mistakes."

"Yeah, but the older we get, the harder and harder it is to justify those mistakes. You want to be able to say that you were young and dumb, but what about when you're old and you're supposed to be smarter?"

"You have a story for us," Amara said, smiling over her tea. And then giving such a sweet loving look at the baby at Olive's feet that Olive wanted to reach over and grab her sister's hand, squeezing it and thanking her for just accepting her baby without needing a big long explanation of what had happened.

"Well, I guess you all know that I did a lot of traveling around the world. I didn't have a whole lot of money, and I didn't want to take the time to get a 'real' job, because so often your money is sucked down in rent and all the things that you get when you decide to put down roots."

"All the things you get you don't really need. I certainly have been there," Amara said, with no sense of judgment at all.

"Well, it wasn't like I avoided all the pitfalls, I spent a lot of money on recreation, having a good time, transportation to get from one place to the next, but I didn't spend a lot of money on things that I didn't think were important, like rent or a wardrobe of clothes, or a car of my own." She didn't mention all the times she'd hitchhiked, grabbed a ride with someone she barely knew, and did all kinds of other dangerous things that she really shouldn't have done. It was funny that God protected her through all of that.

"But the globe-trotting pace was getting a little bit rough and the wanderlust was wearing off, and after our parents died, I spent a lot of time considering coming back for good. The problem was, I had already met a man in Ecuador, who seemed like he shared my values and that we would be good together, but... Anyway, he is the father of Livvy, and when our parents died and I came back, he was waiting for me in Ecuador. I think he saw me as his ticket to the US. He didn't know about the baby before I left, and when I told him about it when I got back, he...disappeared."

"Well, if you thought you were his ticket to the US, a baby would have helped his case."

"Sure. If he hadn't been married. I think one of his friends told him that there was going to be an investigation, and he would have to prove that he wasn't married, and that is what scared him off, more than the baby, but maybe he would have stayed with me if it hadn't been for Livvy." She didn't know that for sure. He had said he wanted to go to the US, but he was content with her in Ecuador. She had taken a job housekeeping at a big resort and had been happy in the hut that she had shared with her boyfriend.

She knew it was wrong and wished that she could erase that part of her life, but like she had just told her sisters, it was there to stay. And she just had to live with it.

"That stinks. And then you had all that trouble getting your plane tickets out."

"Actually, what happened was I got malaria."

Her sisters gasped.

Mertie was the first to recover. "Why didn't you tell us?" It was the kind of voice Olive remembered from their childhood, the commanding voice that did not even consider that she might ask a question and someone might choose not to answer it.

"I didn't want to worry anyone. Ecuador's a long way away, and it's not an easy country to get into and move around in. It's not exactly safe either. I didn't want you to worry about me and end up flying down. Especially after I got the idea that I'd wanted to get closer to you after our parents died. I could hardly do that if you die coming down to try to save my life." Livvy fussed a little, and Olive used her foot to rock the car seat.

She settled almost immediately. She wasn't the kind of baby that was difficult to deal with.

"That must have been terrible to be so sick so far away from home, although you've been trotting around the globe so much that you probably don't even consider the United States your home anymore," Amara said with a little smile. It wasn't exactly a question, but she did have inquiry on her face.

"No. Raspberry Ridge is home. And always has been. And that's why I'm back, although I doubt I can stay. I'm going to need a job, and they're not exactly numerous in small towns like this."

"Oh. When we were talking earlier, I was thinking that maybe you didn't know."

Olive glanced at Amara, her brows drawing down. "Didn't know what?"

"Didn't know about the money that we're getting from our parents' business."

"Yeah," Mertie said. "I didn't realize about it at first either, but it's a good bit of money, and it's going to be a monthly thing."

"A good bit?" Olive said, hope rising in her breast. She had thought that she was only going to be staying here for a little while, as long as her sisters would let her hang out at the mansion before they sold it.

She had figured that she was going to need to get a job in order to pay her way, buy things for her baby, and just live. The United States wasn't like other countries where it didn't take a whole lot to eat every day. Just groceries in the States could suck up more money than she wanted to admit. Maybe the money from her parents would be enough. From the expressions on Mertie's and Amara's faces, it was a good bit.

"It's more than six figures annually."

"No way!" Olive said. That was like a godsend.

"Yeah. We're still trying to iron out the details. It got caught up in a little red tape, and one of the executors wasn't being honest with us. They were diverting the money to somewhere else, but we're on it, so it's going to start, but...not right away."

Olive deflated just a bit. She had next to nothing in her bank account. Third world countries were cheaper to live in, but once a person came back to the United States, they didn't exactly have a nest egg. Not unless they were doing business in the US while living abroad.

"How long do you think?"

"The last time I talked to the attorney, it was going to be at least two months, but he was honestly just giving his best guess. It just depends on how long it takes things to roll through the court and for everything to get straightened out. I honestly don't understand it all."

"Our parents had some complicated things. But the sale of the house should be helpful. I had wanted to buy it myself, but Hobert wants to live down by the lake, and I have to agree. It's so beautiful there, and I think I'd really like to raise my kids down there by the water."

"Wow. That seems so surreal. My big-shot Chicago executive sister is going to be living in a small house down by the lake with Hobert Gilchrest."

She still couldn't wrap her mind around it. It was so crazy. One of those shocking things that almost had to be true.

"And I need to talk to Garnet, but I doubt he is interested in buying it either. He's living with his parents to help them out, and I'm guessing that that's where we're going to live. It's a big old house and they have plenty of room, and his dad needs constant care. So I'm sure I'll be helping with that or giving his mom a break in the kitchen."

The idea of Mertie, Christian speaker and author, who had never wanted to do anything else, cooking and cleaning in a kitchen and taking care of her husband's elderly parents was also almost too far out to be believed.

"You guys have changed so much."

"Following the Lord does that. He changes your life, changes your heart, changes the things that you want, until you are shocked at the fact that you love things you used to hate, and the things that you used to love with all your heart no longer hold any appeal." Mertie said this with complete confidence and no sense of irony in the fact that she was giving up a very lucrative, very promising career to stay at home and be a wife and mom.

"The Bible calls women to be keepers of the home. I know that our society has everything mixed up and backward, but I feel like that's the highest calling for a woman. To minister to her family and to change the course of the world, one family at a time. I think women have been shortchanged by the lie society feeds them." Amara lifted a shoulder. "I know I feel like I was. Being a big-shot executive in Chicago made me feel stressed and hassled, and I actually had an appointment to go to my counselor to be medicated, because I wasn't able to handle it. It's so much more relaxing and so much less stressful here. I wouldn't change it for anything."

She believed that and thought about how the Lord worked. Making it so that Amara ended up not needing the medication after all.

"Well, maybe that's why I'm back in Raspberry Ridge. I was a little disillusioned with my globe-trotting lifestyle. It wasn't as satisfying as I thought it was going to be. I longed for home so much, and after having my daughter, I wanted to make sure that I raised her where she would be sure to pick up the values and morals that small towns have. That's more important than any kind of education she might get from traveling. Although, I would like to travel. Just not for months and months at a time."

$$Five$$

"Months? You mean years," Amara said, giving Olive a playful slap on her forearm. "There were times I had no idea where you were."

"That was the other thing. I really wanted to know my family. I think Mom and Dad's death brought that home even more. I have no idea who they were."

"I didn't really know them either. Kind of makes me sad." Amara looked down at her lap.

"I feel like that's their fault. But you're right, I didn't know them, either. I wish I would have. And all the good memories that I have are associated with this town. Why would I live somewhere else? Why would I think that I can build something better? I just want to be happy with simple things. With ministering beside my husband." When Mertie said 'beside her husband,' her face broke out into a huge smile, and her eyes got the kind of glow that a woman who was in love had.

"It's too bad the three of us can't do something together," Olive said, thinking that she still needed a job for a couple of months. Maybe she wouldn't be able to be back to stay until the inheritance kicked in. She could hardly ask her sisters to spot her until then. Well, she could, but she didn't want to. The bond they were forming was more important to her than anything, and borrowing money from someone didn't exactly scream let's build a bond and get closer. It just meant that the other person was wondering whether it would get paid back, and the borrower was wishing they didn't have to.

"Maybe we can," Mertie said, putting her finger on her chin and thinking. "Everyone has businesses online nowadays. Surely there is something that the three of us could do together that would help us grow closer to each other and also make us money at the same time." Then she laughed. "All right. Maybe we should just be thinking about something that would bring us closer together, and I need to shut off the business part of my brain."

"You and me both. I had the same thought. We could start a business together. But I don't want that stress. And I don't need it. I want to be available any time Hobert wants me to go on the boat with him. That's part of why I quit my job in Chicago. So I didn't have to be tied down."

Olive kept quiet. She really wanted them to get something started, so she didn't have to... She wasn't even sure. She didn't have enough money to put a down payment to rent an apartment, and she was going to have to give her borrowed car back. She basically had nothing, and it felt like a very long, hard road to get her head even above water, let alone having a stable life for her child. Maybe she should have given her up for adoption, but not in Ecuador.

"How hard was it to give your baby up? I mean, not the emotional impact, but red tape wise?"

"Garnet handled most of it," Mertie said immediately, her voice sad and thoughtful. "I just basically dumped her on him, and he reached out to me a few times for some signatures and that type of thing, and he handled it all. I guess I really can't tell you."

She shrugged and then looked down at her drink, swirling the ice in the glass and listening to the clinking sound.

"I might have to do that." There. She got the words out in the open; it wasn't an easy thing to say or admit, but it was true. She wasn't even sure she could take care of herself, let alone her baby. She didn't know why she thought she would arrive in Raspberry Ridge and magically everything would be okay.

"Why?" Mertie and Amara said immediately, looking up at her in surprise and shock.

"I mean we have that money from our parents, you're going to be rolling in it." Amara's face held concern.

"But I don't have anything now."

"You have a car," Mertie started, as though she were listing off all the things that Olive had so she could figure out what they needed and what they could do with what they had.

"It's a borrowed car. I have to have it back by the end of the week."

"Oh," Mertie said.

"How much do you have in your bank account?" Amara asked. "If you don't mind me asking," she added quickly.

She was the one who had brought up the subject, so if they asked questions, she ought to at least be willing to answer them. And she had to admit, it felt good to be talking to her sisters about it.

"I don't have anything," she said, hating that when the words came out, her stomach clenched.

She had rededicated her life to the Lord, but she hadn't gotten a hold of this not fearing thing. She was scared to death about the future. Scared that she was going to lose her daughter or not be able to take care of her.

"That's the last can of formula I have." She didn't mean to be all gloom and doom, but it was the truth.

"Don't worry about that. I...have a little bit of a nest egg, and I'm pretty sure that Garnet is not going to want to start his ministry here in Raspberry Ridge by allowing his sister-in-law to starve. So, what's ours is yours."

"No. I don't want to do that. I don't want to live off of you guys. I want to have a family relationship with you, not a parasitic relationship."

"You would do the same for me."

"Yeah. Except I've been traveling so long, I didn't even know you needed help with your baby."

"That was long before you were trotting the globe. And I know you would have helped me if I asked. I just couldn't ask. It's...not easy." Mertie's voice softened. "I really understand that."

"I appreciate the fact you do, so...maybe you could help me get a job. Or let me work somehow. But I can't just take money."

"All right. We'll figure something out. Garnet has a unique position in the community, and if there are job openings, I'm sure he's probably going to hear about them. That's one thing that a pastor does get—all the gossip. Hopefully he doesn't pass it along though, not the salacious type anyway."

"Amen," Mertie said, and while she was grinning, there was a serious look on her face.

"We don't want a pastor like that, but I don't think we have to worry about Garnet. He's so reliable and upright."

"Any man can fall," Mertie said softly. "But I have as much faith in him as I do in anyone. More actually. He's a good man."

For some reason, those words made Olive sad. Why couldn't she find a good man? Why, after all her years of traveling around the globe, resisting the advances of scores of men, had she fallen for someone who was not just married but a liar as well, ready to ditch her at the slightest hint of trouble? She'd really picked a winner.

Frustrated with herself, scared, and unsure, she set her glass down on the table in front of her.

"I was going to go to the church to pray earlier. I think it's probably cleared out by now, and unless you guys have more things you want to talk about, I kind of would like to take a walk."

She reached down to pick up the car seat where her baby slept.

"If you don't mind, maybe I can watch her sometime? I just... I'm an aunt, two times over, and I just found out about both of them."

"Yes, absolutely." But she didn't suggest that Amara do it just then. Maybe it was because she'd just been thinking she should have given her baby up. She hated the thought - it tore her up inside and she wanted her baby close.

"I'm sorry you didn't know about Dabney," Mertie said as soon as Olive answered. Then she shifted. "I actually have some phone calls I need to think about. And make first thing tomorrow. I might be able to get away with sending a couple of emails, but there are some people I need to talk to. Winding down a ministry is going to mean that there are going to be some people out of jobs, which I hate, but... I know this is the decision I need to make."

"I don't understand why you couldn't continue in that ministry and still marry Garnet." It was true, Olive had no idea why she actually needed to quit her ministry. In fact, it seemed like a silly thing to do. To give up the opportunity to be making money. Olive hadn't seen any numbers, but she was pretty sure that the Raspberry Ridge pastorate didn't pay a whole lot.

"Because when I do something, I put everything I have into it. Everything. And if I'm going to have a ministry, I'm going to throw myself into it with my whole heart and soul. I can't do that and raise a child as well. Can't do that and be a pastor's wife. I... I had to make a choice, and honestly, it wasn't even that hard."

She nodded, still not understanding but not wanting to question her sister either.

Maybe it was just something that she had to live through herself, or maybe when she needed it, God would change her heart. After all, when she was trotting around the globe, she couldn't imagine someone wanting to stay in one place for very long, but now, she had absolutely zero desire to continue traveling and only wanted to put roots down. Preferably with a house and somewhere she could raise her daughter. It was true God took away desires that didn't align with His will at times. Of course, she knew other people who struggled all their lives with desires that were not right and were obviously not things that God wanted.

Lord, why have You helped me so freely, while other people struggle?

It was one of the reasons that she had known that there was a God, because He came to her aid so quickly. Answering her requests. If she didn't have her prayers answered, would she still believe in God?

Or maybe she should ask, if God said no to her requests, since God always answered prayer.

She wasn't sure. She hoped that God gave her a chance to get a little more grounded in Christianity before she had to go through a trial like that.

"Are you okay with her?" Amara asked as Olive picked up the car seat and turned toward the door.

"Yes. I guess I just want to be close to her right now." She didn't try to explain how she felt after thinking about giving her baby up. She couldn't put that terrible feeling into words.

"We might mosey on down to Fran's store and see if she has some formula."

"You don't need to buy formula for me."

"It's a gift for my sister and my niece. Plus, if I can afford to do it, and someone needs it, it's a sin for me not to. James says, 'Therefore to him that knoweth to do good, and doeth it not, to him it is sin.'"

Wow. "How did you even know that was in the Bible?"

"You can't really know what's in the Bible unless you're reading it, can you?"

"I've read it, and I never saw that verse."

"It's kind of funny how sometimes when you're reading, certain verses jump out at you. I think that's how you know that it's the Bible, first of all, and secondly, sometimes God will speak to you through the verses He has you see."

That was something else she wanted to add to her list of things that she was going to do, start reading her Bible more. Every day.

So many things, so many ways she wanted to improve her life, and she felt like she'd wasted so much of it.

But it wasn't wasted if she used the lessons that she learned from doing the wrong thing to help her do the right thing and maybe even show others how to do the right thing. If she used those lessons to point her in the direction that she needed to go and allowed them to remind her that she didn't want to be that person anymore.

"I'll be back," she said before she walked out the door.

Six

Mertie twisted her phone in her hand and looked at Amara, who sat holding her tea and staring off into space.

Maybe she was adjusting to the idea that she had not one, but two nieces.

Mertie found it hard to believe that she not only had a daughter, she had a niece. She felt like her life had been giving her whiplash, yanking her from one spot to another, with new revelation after new revelation. She wouldn't mind having it settle down some and become normal, even boring.

"Do you mind if I go?"

"I can't believe you stayed this long. I know you have some things to talk to Dabney about, and I just want you to know I'm praying for you. I'm confident that conversation is going to go well."

"I wish I was. I'm definitely not, but I hope it does."

Boy, did she ever. It was probably going to be one of the most important conversations of her life. It would affect the way her relationship with her daughter went for years, if not forever.

She wanted to handle it right, wanted more than anything to handle it correctly.

Standing up, she took her glass to the kitchen, rinsed it out, and put it in the dishwasher.

She hurried out the door and down the driveway. She walked, thinking that she might need the exercise to try to clear her head and figure out what she was going to say. But all she could seem to manage to do was to just pray, *Lord, help me. Help Dabney to love me and forgive me for what I've done.*

That was probably as good as anything. Planned speeches didn't always go over very well. At least for her, when she was standing in front of a crowd of people, they always went well, because she could organize her thoughts and power through the speech. When prepared remarks were given in a conversation, though, sometimes she felt like she needed to finish her remarks instead of going with the flow of the conversation.

That didn't always have the desired effect.

It felt like forever, and like no time at all, until she found herself standing beside Garnet's front porch. It was his parents' house, and he lived there with Dabney. She was a little sad that Dabney was her child, and yet Garnet got to live with her. Of course, Garnet had raised her, had adopted her; he had earned the right to live with her.

She tried not to castigate herself too badly over that, but she didn't think she would ever get rid of the guilt she felt for not being there for her child, even though she was not prepared in any way to be raising a child. Of course, Garnet hadn't been either.

Maybe Garnet and Dabney had been waiting for her, since they were sitting outside on the porch swing.

"Hey there." She wanted to talk to Garnet too. Tell him what an awesome job he had done today. That he had preached another sermon that had hit directly in her heart and made her want to be a better person. Was there a better sermon than that? One that inspired a person to want to make changes in their life, changes that brought them to the Lord, inspired them to be closer to Him, and helped their relationship?

She would rather hear a sermon like that any day of the week than a sermon that just told her what she already knew or what she wanted to hear, assuring her she was fine and there was no need to upset the apple cart by trying to do anything new.

She'd heard too many of those sermons in her life before, though she had highly doubted that she would hear too many more, if she was going to get married to Garnet and sit under his preaching for the rest of her life. The idea was still new, but it also sent a thrill of excitement down her spine.

"Hey. We've been waiting on you."

"I got away as soon as I could. I... I know that Olive is going to the church, so do you mind if we talk here?"

"I think this is a perfect place," Garnet said, and then he looked over at Dabney, who nodded. She looked a little shy, meeting Mertie's eyes for a quick second before she looked down, dragging her toe on the porch as Garnet pushed the swing back and forth.

There were three rocking chairs, and she chose the one that was closest to the swing. She loved this front porch. It was beautiful, everything that a small-town porch should be, and she felt completely content as she sat down.

At least physically she felt content. Emotionally she was all tied up, even though she knew that God was in control, and He would make the conversation go the way it needed to go, even if it wasn't the way she wanted it to. Even if it meant a lifetime of struggle and strife and pain between her daughter and her. If that was God's will, she didn't want it, but she would accept it and live through it because God knew best.

With those thoughts, that God was in control, and she just needed to submit to His will, and it didn't really depend on her, she felt her insides relaxing.

She was the kind of person who liked to take things and manipulate them until they fit what she wanted. That worked whenever she was building her ministry or any other kind of business, but when a person was trying to live a life submitted to the Lord's will, it made things a little bit hard for them. She had probably struggled more than the average person to pry her fingers up and just give God control.

"I guess I don't know where to start," she said when no one else said anything.

"Are we talking about the fact that you gave me up for adoption?" Dabney asked, and Mertie realized that they hadn't really said exactly what they were going to sit down and talk about.

"That's what I was hoping to talk about. I wanted to kind of explain to you why." She looked around. "Are your parents awake?" she asked Garnet.

"No. Mom just went in half an hour ago to take a nap, and Dad's been sleeping for at least twice that long."

She nodded. "All right. Not that I care. Everyone's going to know. But I wanted to talk to Dabney about it before I send any emails to anyone or make any phone calls tomorrow."

"Why?" Dabney asked suddenly. She'd had a little while to think about it. She had found out she was adopted when she realized how much she looked like Mertie a few weeks ago and wondered if Mertie might indeed be her mother. She had asked Helen, Garnet's mother, and Helen had told her the whole story.

Dabney had just been waiting for Mertie and Garnet to tell her, and when they didn't, she finally asked them when they were going to.

"I'm sorry I didn't tell you earlier. I... I guess I felt like I didn't really have that right anymore."

Garnet's jaw tightened, and she could tell he didn't like what she said, but he didn't interrupt her.

"I gave you up for adoption. And I suppose that means that whoever adopted you has the right to decide what happens to you, at least until you're old enough to make those decisions for yourself."

"Which, I'm almost old enough," Dabney said, sounding every second of her fourteen years.

"You certainly are, honey. And you're mature for your age. You have always handled any responsibility that I've given you, which tells me that you can handle more." Garnet spoke softly, but not long, almost as though he knew this conversation was one that needed to be between Dabney and Mertie. "In fact, if you'd like me to, I can leave. So that you and your mother can talk without me."

"I'd like you to stay," Dabney said immediately.

"Me too," Mertie said, meaning it. It wasn't that she was afraid to talk to Dabney by herself, that wasn't exactly it, but she did feel a certain amount of support and encouragement and confidence when Garnet was around.

"Are you going to answer me?" Dabney asked softly, quietly, not defiantly, not angrily, but determined to get her answers.

The question made Garnet smile just a bit, and she could almost hear him saying, "she has a bit of you in her." Which would be true. Any determination or stubbornness she had, she most definitely got from Mertie.

"I didn't think I could keep you. I didn't think I could give you a good life. I was a student, I made some bad choices, choices I wish I could go back and undo. Except, that means I wouldn't have you, and I suppose in every regret there's a rainbow, if you want to look at it like that, and you are the rainbow. So, maybe I wouldn't undo it. But I do regret it. And I definitely regret giving you up. I would like to go back and tell myself that I could have done it."

"But if you'd done that, not given me up, I wouldn't have Dad."

"Exactly. And you have the best dad in the whole world. I can't think of another person who could be a better dad to you. And I think that's one thing I did right."

"I guess I was thinking about that. I mean, I've always wanted a mom. Always. I wished I had one, I longed for one, but knowing that for you to keep me meant Dad wouldn't get me, and I wouldn't have Dad, I guess... The only way I would have wanted you to keep me would have been if you and Dad would have been together."

Mertie nodded, waiting until Dabney looked down at her lap before she shifted her eyes and met Garnet's gaze.

They were together now, planning a marriage.

"I wish I would have been that smart back then. Your dad actually suggested that, and I said no way. I thought we were too young to get married. I thought I was too young to be a wife and a mom, to give you a good upbringing, but... I think that would have been the better way to go. But I guess that's what I wanted to talk to you about today. I can't undo the past. I can't go back and try to figure out a better way. I did the best that I knew how to do at the time. The best for you, and I just hope that you can forgive me, and we can have a relationship from now on."

"When you and Dad get married?"

"Yeah. And now, too. Because I don't know how long it's going to be."

"Soon?"

"As soon as he'll marry me." She smiled a little, not liking the unknowns in that equation either. Her controlling personality wanted to twist everything so that it did what she wanted it to do, rather than the way it would play out over time.

"I'll marry you tonight if we can."

"I think we need a license. That would be a few days anyway."

She noticed that Dabney had not said that she forgave her. Was that because Dabney didn't feel like there was anything to forgive? She had hinted at that when she had said that she wouldn't want Mertie to do anything different if it meant she wasn't going to have Garnet as a dad, or did that mean that Dabney wasn't yet ready to talk about forgiveness?

The idea made Mertie bite her lips, but she wasn't going to press. Although, she supposed asking one more time wouldn't be pressing too hard.

"I was thinking about getting Pastor Calvin to marry us," Garnet said, with his brows raised as though asking her.

"I think that would be really nice," she said, knowing he was talking about the pastor that they had growing up, and she would love to have him marry them, although he was in an assisted living facility. His wife, Mrs. Calvin, had been where Mertie had gone in order to hide her pregnancy. She had a deep affection for the couple; they were tied to some of the best and worst memories of her life.

"I'll ask and see what he says. I actually have a wedding to perform—your sister and Hobert."

"I know. I was talking to her about that today. I was kind of wondering who would get married first."

"I think it should be us. Then I'll be the pastor of the church when I marry them. That just seems like a better order than trying to get things cattywampus. I think they'll be willing to wait a couple of weeks."

"I don't know. They're pretty impatient."

"I might be a little impatient too." He smiled with so much tenderness she felt it the whole way to her bones.

"I've been waiting for this all my life." She hadn't even known it. She'd been waiting to have a man who adored her, who wanted her for who she was, who would be a great husband and father. She'd already seen what a great dad he was, so that was not even something she questioned.

It was almost like sampling the goods before she got them, only in the very best way.

"You didn't answer me when I asked if you thought you could forgive me, Dabney," she said again, turning her head to Dabney and focusing on what she had gone there for. She knew that Garnet and she could work things out. They were both in the Christian ministry, and they both wanted to live their lives pleasing to the Lord.

She didn't want to get complacent though. Just because both of them were Christians, just because both of them wanted to do what God wanted them to do, didn't mean that their relationship wouldn't need constant work the way relationships always did. In her heart, she wanted to do the work, but she knew that often the work was hard things, like forgiving, letting go, giving in when she felt like her way was best, letting someone else take the credit, serving without reward, and following her husband, and for her, the challenges would be even greater because of her husband being in the ministry. As a pastor, his people would expect him to be there for them when they were having babies, funerals, and illnesses and crises in their home.

She had to be able to share her husband, not feel neglected, and support him however she could. She wasn't blind to the challenges, since she'd been in the ministry and knew what it contained.

Was she up for it?

That really wasn't the question. The question was, was she going to be able to follow the Lord as He led her down this path? Because with God, she didn't need her strength, she only needed His.

The seconds ticked by as she held her breath, waiting for Dabney to answer her.

But Dabney appeared confused. "What do I have to forgive you for?"

"For giving you away." She thought it was obvious.

"We just said, if you hadn't given me up, I wouldn't have Dad. God worked it out perfectly. Dad took care of me until you and Dad met up again, and now I have a mom. I mean, I still wish I would have had a mom all of my life, but getting one late is better than never getting one."

Mertie had to laugh.

Garnet said, "Better late than never; you could have made up the saying."

"Yeah. That saying. Better late than never. It applies to my mom."

She couldn't believe that that was it. Maybe other things would come up at some point. Maybe she would have it tossed in her face that she had given her up whenever they were arguing sometime in the future, but for now, she couldn't believe how good God had been to her. He had worked everything out.

"Is it okay with you if your mother and I get married?"

"I want that," Dabney said. "Didn't I suggest it?"

Was that how it happened? She supposed, as a woman, she should be upset that it didn't seem like Garnet wanted her until his daughter asked her, but she knew that wasn't the way it was at all. Garnet wouldn't have asked her until he knew for sure that his daughter was okay with it. Perhaps if Dabney was out of the house, married, and on her own, then her opinion wouldn't be so important. But Mertie hoped that they were a close-knit family and that getting permission was just something they all did.

She supposed having a family that was close was something that had to be worked on as well. And now that she didn't have her career to focus on, she could put all of her energy into doing the very best that she could for her family and for her husband and their church.

She couldn't wait to get started.

But first, she had some phone calls she had to make. Tomorrow.

Seven

D oyle bit back a word he shouldn't say as he accidentally grabbed the pan without an oven mitt.

It was too late to salvage the food anyway. The fish he had been cooking in the oven had been burnt to a crisp.

He'd have to redouble his efforts to find a housekeeper/cook. Someone who was willing to do it all. In this huge house, set a half a mile back off the road in Raspberry Ridge, he could even offer them a room, as long as they were okay staying with a complete stranger.

But if he didn't do something soon, he was going to starve to death. This was the fourth time this week he'd had to either skip supper or go somewhere to find some.

Deciding that he'd try the little store on Main Street, to see if she had gotten in anything other than the chips and soda he'd had for supper yesterday, he shut the oven off, ran some cold water over his hand until it quit burning, and grabbed his keys.

This house he was renting was a beautiful house, although it needed some updates. That's what his sister would have said, but Doyle didn't really care. He did like things to be tidy, and knickknacks and clutter bothered him, but outdated appliances? Not so much. Maybe the floor could use a good cleaning, or they could pull the carpet up and put some tile or hardwood or something down, but he didn't want it bad enough that he was actually going to try to figure out what needed to be done, and then figure out how to hire someone, and whether or not they were trustworthy, and go through all of that rigmarole.

He had a business to run, and ironically it was managing rental properties. But mostly he just managed people, the people who managed the rental properties. They were the ones who found the folks who did the updates or even the folks who told them what the updates needed to be. He didn't have to worry himself with any of that, thankfully.

All of that was just a jumble in his head, trying to keep him from thinking about the things that he most wanted to think about.

Olive.

He wanted to be able to get her out of his head, to shove her aside and not wonder if she was still in town, wonder if she had maybe come back for him. He hadn't seen a husband. Maybe... No, the baby was too young.

It didn't matter. He wasn't interested anyway.

Deciding that he was too hungry to walk, he got in his car and drove to Fran's. What this town needed was a good restaurant. Except, they needed a little bit more tourist traffic before a restaurant could stay in business. He was enough of a business owner to know that much. He didn't know anything about restaurants though.

Parking along the street, he was out of his car before he realized that the figure walking down from the church was familiar. Not just familiar; it was Olive.

Did he wait and try to talk to her? Or did he run into the store and pretend he didn't see her?

Wasn't it sad that he was even thinking about which of the two choices he should make?

"Doyle! I've been thinking about you." Pastor Garnet, smiling from ear to ear with his arm wrapped around the woman who had stood beside him in church earlier that morning, called his name from across the road. They looked both ways, although why they did, he wasn't sure, since there was never any traffic in Raspberry Ridge, and hurried across.

"Hey, Pastor Garnet, Miss Mertie," he said. His stomach growled, reminding him of his errand, but it would be rude to not stand and chat for at least a couple of minutes. "What were you thinking about?" He highly doubted that the pastor had any properties that needed to be managed, and the only other thing might be that he wanted Doyle to do some kind of job in the church.

Doyle was perfectly willing. He wanted to do what he could to serve the Lord, around the job he had. He figured it probably should be the other way around, his job came second to whatever he was doing for God, but in a town like Raspberry Ridge, and a church as small as what they had, there wasn't exactly a whole pile of demands on his time.

Still, he didn't want to be standing there when Olive hit the sidewalk, which was just a matter of seconds.

"Well, I actually had someone that might make a good housekeeper for you, but I haven't had a chance to say something to her." He paused. "But God's timing is better than mine, and when I saw Olive coming down the hill and you parking in front of the store, I figured that I'd just go with the flow and go with God's timing."

A very bad feeling started to gather in his stomach, but his brain was moving so slowly he couldn't quite figure out exactly what it was.

"Okay?" he said instead, slowly, like he was talking from a distance and the words in his brain couldn't reach his mouth without hopping over air.

"So there's Olive right now, and we can see what she says. I might have solved your problem, or maybe I should put it more like God might have solved your problem, and He just used me as the facilitator."

If he wasn't the pastor, Doyle might have said he didn't have any problems that were that big that he needed Olive in order to solve them, but he didn't want to be rude to the new pastor. Not only did he want to start out on the right foot and stay on the pastor's good side, but he also wanted to be a good Christian, and it probably started with being kind to the pastor.

But he didn't really have time to think of a way out or to even turn and run. Because Olive was there. She didn't look any more thrilled to see him than he was to see her, but Pastor Garnet didn't seem to notice.

Mertie might have been another story, but Doyle wasn't really looking at her, because his eyes were caught by Olive. She carried the carseat, which seemed like it was too heavy for her, and she looked sallow and sickly. Her clothes hung on her body, and she was walking slowly. Like she'd been sick.

Had she been sick?

Pastor Garnet spoke to her. "This is Doyle McKenny. I don't know if you remember him, but he's looking for a housekeeper. And your sister told me that you might be looking for a job. I was kind of excited to see the two of you together. And felt like that just might be the Lord working there."

Olive's mouth opened and closed several times, and if Doyle hadn't been pretty sure that his mouth was doing the same thing, he might have laughed at her. She looked ridiculous, but he probably did too.

"I..." she began, but Mertie cut in.

"I know you were just saying today how much you wanted to have a job. You might only need it for two months, so you have to be upfront about that, of course, but it would at least give Doyle time to find someone who's willing to move the whole way up here, into a small town, where they'll have to drive to get anywhere."

"I mean, that is okay with you, Doyle, right? You asked me if I knew anyone, and I'm telling you I do. Maybe I should have checked with you first?" Pastor Garnet's voice started to slow down and soften, like he realized that maybe he had stepped into a situation that he hadn't anticipated and didn't know exactly what was going on.

Doyle shook his head. "No. I did ask you. I'm actually here in town tonight because I ruined supper. Again."

He wasn't sure, but he thought that maybe Olive snorted.

When he turned his head to look at her though, she was looking at the ground. As though thinking.

"Well then, there you go, Olive. Doyle needs a housekeeper and a cook, and you can do both. Even with the baby," Mertie said.

It made Doyle flinch. So there really was a baby. It was there in the car seat. He hadn't imagined that, and it was hers.

His face tightened.

"Is that going to be a problem?" Pastor Garnet asked.

He paused. It was going to be a problem. But only if he let it. He could handle this. He could do this without it causing a major upheaval in his life. He'd just avoid her. She could cook, she could clean, she could go home.

"I was under the impression that you might have a place for her to live too. Not that she can't live at the mansion. She wants to, but we're trying to get it cleaned out so we can get it on the market. And then she would be out of the home. So if you have a room, and I understand you do, that would be perfect."

"Two rooms, if she wants a separate room for the baby. I…" What was he saying? Why had he agreed to that? He didn't want her there.

"We could stay in the same room. And yes. I'll take the job if Doyle will hire me."

Doyle stared. His last hope was that she would turn him down, decide that it wasn't what she wanted, and that she didn't want to be with him, that she was just as loath to live under the same roof as him as he was to live under the same roof as her.

"I'm willing." He wasn't going to let it be said that he was the one who wouldn't take the help that was offered.

They paused in their conversation as a car drove slowly down, then took the turn to go back toward his house. His was the only house back there, although the lane went farther back to an overlook that was three quarters of a mile or so from his house. But no one ever went there anymore. It was on the same property, and there were signs out past the house warning people that it was private.

Most of the people who didn't live in Raspberry Ridge had totally forgotten about it. But that must be where the car was going.

Regardless, he looked back at the group of people gathered around him, realizing that everything that he had been thinking today, how he was going to stay away from Olive, how if she stayed in Raspberry Ridge, he would have to go, how it was hard to avoid people in a small town, but he could manage it since he worked from home and spent most of his daylight time in his office, dealing with things. How he would just avoid her and hope that she was leaving soon. All of that had been wasted time.

Since now here he stood, just agreeing to hire her. And not just hire her but house her under the same roof as him. Not only her, but her and her *baby*.

Yeah. Fat lot of good all the stuff that he had thought about all day had done him. He might as well have been thinking about something constructive.

"All right then, If you'd like her to start, she's available whenever."

"She also has her own mouth and can finish the negotiations from here." Olive spoke up, not sounding terribly upset, maybe even having a bit of humor in her voice. He wanted her to be angry, he wanted her to say no way, that she wasn't going to do it, but he was the one who had been hurt and betrayed by her, both when she left and when she came back. He was the one who should have opened his mouth and said it wasn't something he was going to do. But he hadn't.

"All right then, you two take over and let us know if there's anything more we can do to help." Garnet grinned and squeezed the woman beside him. She looked up at him with an adoring look before they walked on down the road and went into Fran's store, the bells tinkling overhead.

Well, the thing he did not want most had happened. He supposed all that was left was to deal with it.

Eight

What had she been thinking?

No, she had no money, no house, just relying on her sisters' goodwill, and even then she would be in the way as they tried to clean the mansion up to get it ready to sell. She had no choice but to take the first job that was offered, even if it was offered by Doyle McKenny.

She wasn't sure exactly what God was thinking on that one, but her faith that God knew best wasn't wavering. However, her faith that she would be able to do what God wanted her to do was at an all-time low. Or maybe it was just stuck in the trenches where it had always been. She never really thought of herself as someone who could follow God and do what He wanted. She just wasn't that kind of person.

But she wanted to be.

And just like Rome wasn't built in a day, she wasn't going to be the kind of person she wanted to be overnight. And she was never going to become that person if she didn't start making herself do things that were a little bit hard.

Like taking a job with the one man in the entire world that she was trying to avoid.

Her sister and Garnet walked away, and the silence stretched between Doyle and herself.

She felt like she should break it, except he was the one who had hired her. Didn't he have instructions or something for her? Or maybe an application to fill out? Or maybe once her sister had left, he was going to tell her that he no longer wanted her.

Maybe she should just be the bigger person and tell him that he didn't have to.

"You don't have—"

"I'm sorry about—"

They started together, stopped, and stared at each other some more. Finally he said, "You can go first."

"No. You. I... I appreciate the offer of a job. If you truly mean it."

"I'm not in the habit of saying things I don't mean."

He didn't add, unlike some people I know, which he could have. But Doyle always was mature and didn't go for the cheap shots. Although was it a cheap shot if it was true?

"I've changed." She bit her tongue. She didn't think that you should have to tell a person that you changed. Your actions would show it. That's what she believed and what she wanted to live, but the words were out before she could stop them.

She expected him to smirk and snort and scoff at her declaration, but he just looked sad.

"I think life does change us. And I agree, you're different." He looked down at the car seat by her feet, as though that was the only change in her life. It wasn't what she was talking about at all, but she didn't know how to correct him and figured that it was probably best that she didn't. She hadn't wanted to tell him about the change, she had wanted to show him anyway.

He had always been a strong Christian. She was the one who had been the Christian in name only. But he had loved her anyway.

And she had loved his strong steadiness, even as it repelled her. Maybe because she felt like she just needed to get out and do her own thing. She wanted to have freedom, freedom to make bad choices.

Except bad choices always had consequences, and looking back, she wished she hadn't had that freedom at all. It was foolish of her to think that she needed it, when what she really needed was to be content where she was and follow God wherever He led her.

"So... When were you thinking you wanted me to start?"

"Tonight if possible. I'm in town because I burnt supper."

She looked up, and there seemed to be humor in his eyes. Although his expression was still guarded, like he didn't trust her. And rightfully so. That's what she had taught him. That he couldn't trust her. Because she betrayed him. She had taken the things that he'd given her, his love, his care, his concern, his devotion, and rather than cherish them the way they should have been cherished, she'd thrown it all back in his face, and stomped on it for good measure, and then she left. Making some sort of vague promise that she'd be back eventually. But he shouldn't wait on her. Although he could if he wanted to. And he'd said he would.

He'd kept his word. And she supposed, in a way, she'd kept hers since she was back.

"I can start tonight if you want to. I don't know what kind of groceries you have in your house, but I'm sure I can whip something up."

"You'd probably have a hard time making a meal out of a few sticks of butter and some condiments."

"You're kidding?"

"No. I'm dead serious. I might have a few spices in the cupboard."

"So... We'll have to go grocery shopping first."

"Have you had supper yet?" he asked, and something in his tone made her eyes fly to his.

"No?"

"All right. Let's go grocery shopping, and we'll grab supper on the way."

She swallowed. She didn't want him to be this nice to her. And she definitely didn't want to go out to eat with him. Those days were over. She'd ruined it, and she didn't deserve a second chance.

"How about you just go grocery shopping and let me know when you're going to be home, and I'll meet you there at your house."

She didn't have to ask, because she knew she could stay with her sisters, but she also knew that her sisters were both planning on getting married and moving out and they wanted the house to be empty so they could sell it. So she said, "Is there really room for me?"

"I have a room. One for your kid as well." He didn't sound overly friendly, and the humor that had been in his expression was completely gone.

Had she done it again? Had she taken his olive branch and thrown it back in his face because she wanted to make sure that she wasn't beholden to him or that she had her freedom?

She didn't give herself another chance to second-guess herself, but instead she said, "If it's okay with you, I've changed my mind and I'll go shopping with you. I might have to feed my baby at some point, because she's going to be hungry when she wakes up."

"I haven't seen her do anything but sleep."

She took a breath, realizing at that second that she was going to need to ask for her wages to be paid early. She hated to do that, because he had already done so much for her just by giving her a job. By hiring her on the spot, not making her wait to start. Everything else that she needed she could do without, other than diapers, but she had enough of those to last for a week if she was careful. But formula, she couldn't live without. If she hadn't been so sick after she had the baby, she should have been able to nurse her, but the malaria had made sure that she couldn't.

"I have a favor to ask."

He had started to turn toward his car, but he stopped, lifting a brow. Waiting.

She lifted her chin. "If you buy three cans of formula when you buy your groceries, I'll pay you back when I get paid out of my first check."

He lifted his head slowly and then dropped it, like he was nodding in slow motion or thinking hard.

"That's fine." He took a breath, almost as though he were bracing himself, and then he said, "Anything else?"

She shook her head. "No."

"All right then. I'm starving. Let's go." He walked to his car without waiting for her, but he opened the passenger door, hesitated a moment, and then stepped back and opened the back passenger door as well.

"Is there a trick to putting her in?" he asked as he held his hand out for the car seat.

He was going to put the baby in? She had gotten the impression that he didn't like children and was a little annoyed that she had a baby, but it might have been because of their history.

"Normally there's a base, but that's in my car. It'll be fine without it." Then she explained how he would need to latch the seat belt around the hooks of the car seat and make sure that it was secure.

She didn't mean to stand over his shoulder and watch, but she supposed that she hadn't been a mother long enough for her to just assume that he was going to do it correctly. Or maybe she just liked watching him, not interact with the baby exactly, but take care of her. She always thought he would make a great dad. That opinion had not changed. There was something attractive about a man who was good with children.

He straightened out, saw her watching, and lifted that one brow again. "Did I do it right?"

"You did it perfectly," she said, like she wouldn't have expected anything else from him.

But he just jerked his head and slammed the door shut.

He turned back to her door and held it while she got in. When they had been together, he had always opened her doors and showed her the utmost respect. It was one of the things she loved about him. One of the many things.

She watched as he walked around the front of the car, confident as always, his long legs somehow graceful, his hands at his sides, capable but not threatening. And of course there was that shock of orange hair that not only made him stand out but kept him from looking too austere.

They were quiet as he pulled out, leaving Raspberry Ridge and taking the right turn on the highway south toward Blueberry Beach.

"There's a good diner in Strawberry Sands, but there's no grocery store. I typically pick my things up in Blueberry Beach. Will that work for you?"

"Yeah." Like she would argue about where he should get his groceries. Of course she wasn't going to do that. She would cook what he wanted her to and use whatever foods he bought. All she needed was enough formula to get her through until payday.

"So what brings you back?" he asked, after silence had filled the car for what felt like forever.

"I guess I was just ready to come home." That was the truth, although she could also add that when she was dying in Ecuador, all she could think of was that Doyle would have taken care of her. Even though she had broken up with him, left him, hurt him, she knew all she would have to do would be to pick up the phone, if she actually had service, and call him, and he would come, even to a different country in order to take care of her. That was just the kind of man he was.

"Where's the baby's father?" He sounded like he didn't want to ask that question, but he couldn't stop himself. And she didn't blame him. If he had a child and she didn't see a mother around, that would be the first thing she would want to ask.

"He left when I got sick. I found out later he was married. It was a mistake, obviously."

She couldn't sugarcoat that. She couldn't pretend it didn't happen, and she couldn't pretend she was happy about it. She screwed up. Plain and simple. Sin always seemed so seductive before one fell, and it always felt so vile and terrible when one was spending the rest of their life regretting it.

Of course she wasn't going to regret her daughter, but it was the only good thing that came out of her stupidity and determination to do what she wanted to do instead of what God wanted her to do.

Well, maybe there was one more thing.

"It was the dumbest thing I'd ever done, deliberately knowing that it was wrong. And then I ended up with malaria, and in an Ecuadorian hospital which is...not like American hospitals." To say the least. "But while I was there, I didn't have anyone to depend on except for the Lord. That's what I meant earlier when I said that I had changed. And I suppose that's why I'm back. I'm...not the same girl I was when I left."

She didn't want him thinking that she was trying to talk him into taking her back. Or trying to tell him that she wanted to pick up where they left off because she was different and wouldn't throw away all the precious things that he gave her. But she understood that that was water under the bridge, and a person couldn't go back. Unfortunately. She wished she could. Because maybe more than the sin that she'd done with Ricardo, her biggest mistake was walking away from Doyle.

But it wasn't as big of a mistake if she actually learned something from it, and she had to remember that. She didn't want to start doing okay on her own and walk away from the Lord again. Because that was when the danger was greatest. When things were going well and she felt like she didn't need Him. She'd figured that much out too.

Now, if she could just put those lessons into practice, to make that part of her life worthwhile.

Nine

Doyle pulled into the diner in Blueberry Beach.

He hadn't said much since Olive had admitted that she'd made mistakes. If she thought he was going to take her back just because she came and declared herself a new person, she was dead wrong.

Even though he thought that, he knew he was just showing bravado in his mind. He hadn't stopped loving her simply because she had been unkind and walked away. Just because she hurt him. She was still the same person, sweet and fun, although obviously with a lot more baggage than she used to have.

It made him mad. She could have said yes to him, and none of this would have happened, they could have a few kids of their own, living a quiet life in Raspberry Ridge.

Of course, he wouldn't have gone to Chicago and made some good decisions that had him ending up owning a property management company. He would never have been able to come back, renting a mansion on the outside of town and with the flexibility to work wherever he wanted to.

Still, he hated the fact that Olive had been sick and alone. That she had a child and had been hurt. Even though he was glad all of it had brought her back to God and back to him, too. Except... Did he want to go through that again? Could he trust the fact that she said she changed?

He pulled into the diner and got out, walking around the car, although Olive was out before he reached her door. So he went to the back door and opened it, figuring that it wouldn't be that hard to unlatch the baby.

It didn't take long to eat, and they didn't talk at all other than what was necessary.

The grocery store wasn't that far up the sidewalk, but he drove to it just so they didn't have to carry the bags of groceries back to the car. He wasn't sure how much she was going to get.

"I can carry the baby if you want to push the cart and pick out what you need."

She looked at him with shock in her eyes. "You want me to go shopping?"

"I'll pay for it." He didn't see why she was so surprised. He couldn't pick out the groceries if she was going to be doing the cooking.

"Okay. How many days do you want me to shop for?"

"However many days you want to not have to come back and go grocery shopping again."

"Well," she said as she pulled a cart out of the line of carts at the front of the store. "I don't really have any recipes in my head, so I would want to go home and make a menu for the week and create a list of the groceries that I need to purchase, so how about I get enough for...three days?"

"It's up to you."

He really didn't want to have anything to do with the cooking. "I guess we could have talked about what I was expecting out of you and your job on the way here." He had been too busy thinking about how much he liked her, and still liked her even after what she'd done to him, to be able to actually have a coherent thought about his life and employees apparently. "But I'm hoping that you'll do all the cooking and all the cleaning. All the grocery shopping and all the food prep."

"All right." She paused for a moment, and he didn't expect her to say anything else. What more was there to say?

"I remember that you don't like coconut, and salmon is your

favorite. Is there anything else you absolutely do not want to have? I don't recall you not liking any vegetables."

"I hate peppers."

"Oh, that's right. But you eat onions. In fact, you love them."

"A little too much maybe," he said, and he couldn't keep the smile from turning his lips up. They'd had a couple of discussions about that back in the day.

Her lips turned up as well, and it was almost like they were sharing a moment. Almost, but not quite. Because there was still all of this stuff between them. The hurt and the anger, the betrayal and whatever it was that caused her to walk away from him. Caused him to not be enough for her.

He supposed that he had changed as well, but whether his changes were enough that she would decide to stay were open for interpretation. Or maybe it wasn't. He didn't want to be hurt like that again. Not that he wanted to live his life making his decisions based on fear. He just wanted to be prudent. A person with a heartache wasn't nearly as good of a businessperson and asset to the community as someone who wasn't fighting such a condition.

Still, the fact that she had remembered his likes and dislikes made him feel seen in a way that he hadn't felt since she'd been gone.

She went around the store, like she was used to finding her own groceries, with confidence and careful consideration as she picked up various fruits and vegetables and looked at them. He had no idea what made her put one down and pick another up, but he admired that ability. He supposed that if he worked on it, maybe he could too, but that was the point of hiring someone to do it for him.

They were in the store less than half an hour, and the groceries that she had in her cart didn't look like nearly enough for three days. But she was the one he had hired, and he would defer to her expertise in the area.

They got in the car, with him buckling the baby in, only this time she got in her seat without standing over his shoulder. Maybe she was content that he actually knew what he was doing. He wasn't sure and didn't ask. He just kept getting the feeling that maybe this wasn't such a good idea.

But it felt like God had opened the doors and he just needed to walk through. If that's what it was, he needed to accept it, and if it wasn't, he just needed to keep an eye out for a sign from the Lord that he should be doing something else.

They were about halfway home when she startled him by speaking. "The car that I have is borrowed. I... I'll need to borrow yours in order to go get groceries, and I'll need to have Friday off so that I can take the car back to Ohio to my friend's place."

He didn't say anything for a moment. This was news to him. She truly didn't have anything if she needed to borrow against the wages that she would earn in order to buy formula for her daughter and the car that she drove wasn't even hers. She was truly in bad straits.

His heart wanted to fold over in compassion, but he reminded himself that she was the reason that he'd felt like a zombie for almost a year after she left him.

It was embarrassing to admit that it had taken him that long to want to live again. Not that he was thinking about suicide, but that he just didn't have any motivation to get out of bed. Of course he did it anyway, because he had a job and that's what the human thing was to do.

But he needed his heart to understand that even though the Christian thing was to help her and show compassion, he needed to be reserved, and careful, and not fall again. That would be foolish.

"I'm sorry to ask. I know I haven't even worked a full week, and I just requested a day off, but I do have to get this car back. I promised."

Irritation bubbled inside of him. She made promises to him and hadn't kept them. Or maybe not promises exactly, but she allowed him to think that there was a future for them, when she was just planning on leaving.

"Of course. If you promised, you need to keep that promise." He didn't say any of the other things that were rolling around in his head. He didn't want to be unkind.

"Thank you. So, you want me to cook all the meals and do all the cleaning. Do you have any set times for the meals? Or any specific things you want cleaned more often than others?"

"I'm typically up and have breakfast by six, lunch around twelve, and supper around six, although earlier is better. I don't like to go to bed on a full stomach."

"Me either. When we were younger, none of that stuff seemed to matter, but now..."

"We're not that old." They were barely thirty.

"You know what I mean. Kids can handle anything, but I'm definitely realizing that things change as you get older."

It reminded him that she didn't look that good. Maybe it wasn't a matter of her being older. Maybe it was a matter of her being sick.

"Was malaria all you had?"

"Yeah. It ended up getting a little complicated, not the brain stuff, thankfully but... I fell into a coma, and I ended up being sick for about two months."

"But you're better now?"

She nodded. "Yeah."

He seemed to remember that malaria could flare up again if it wasn't treated properly. And he wondered if maybe hers wasn't. But in Ecuador, surely they were used to treating malaria, and they might even be better at it than a hospital here in the US that didn't see many cases of it. If any.

Still, being sick for two months would explain why she looked so terrible.

"How old's the baby?"

"She's two months. I heard that pregnant women are more susceptible to malaria, and I kinda thought that maybe I was exposed right before I went into labor. I'm not sure. Regardless, she was fine, just... I couldn't feed her, couldn't really hold or do anything with her for the first few weeks. It was...tough."

He could only imagine. Being in a strange country and having no one to help you. "What about the father?"

"I found out about his wife a few days before I went into labor. He wasn't around for any of it and was clear that he didn't want to have anything to do with me or the baby. He couldn't afford to support us was basically what he said."

Yeah. That sounded about right.

He wanted to quit thinking about it, didn't want to have compassion for her, because after all, she was suffering because of her own choices. But he'd made bad choices. He'd made mistakes. And he appreciated when people didn't rub it in his face that he'd been stupid, but instead held out a hand and gave him some help standing back up and getting on his feet.

"Who's bringing you home when you deliver the car?" he asked.

"I don't know. I haven't gotten that far yet. Probably one of my sisters."

"Plan on me."

Yeah. So much for staying away from her. For just letting her do her thing in his house, and he would do his. Except, he couldn't just leave her stranded in Ohio because she had to have a car back. He had to help her. That just made sense.

"Are you sure?" she asked, sounding like she couldn't keep the surprise out of her voice.

"Said I would," he said, not wanting to question why and definitely not wanting her to question his motives. "I guess I know you won't run off on me if I'm following you there and bringing you back." That was a low blow, and he shouldn't have said it, but he didn't want her to get any closer to the truth, which was...he wasn't even sure. He didn't want to let her out of his sight? He didn't want to take a chance that she would leave him again? He rejected both of those ideas, not wanting them to be true, although unable to say for sure that they weren't.

He shouldn't have said anything so unkind. Shouldn't have rubbed it in. He didn't want people to do that to him, and he shouldn't do that to others.

But he didn't take it back, and they rode the rest of the way in silence. It felt heavy and unnatural.

Most of the time that he'd spent with Olive had been fun. They had grown up along the shores of Lake Michigan in Raspberry Ridge together, and although they hadn't been best friends, they'd known each other and played together all their lives. When she'd come back to visit for a summer after she graduated from high school, that was when their romance had really taken off. But that was also when she'd left.

When he first pulled into the drive, he didn't notice anything amiss. Perhaps because he was thinking about the decisions he made over the last several hours and wondering if he'd chosen food over faith. But then, as he pulled the car to a stop, he noticed a figure moving on the porch. It took him a couple of seconds until she moved into the light where he could see her better that he realized it was Cassie, his housekeeper from Chicago.

He'd called and left a message but hadn't heard anything back.

"Am I interrupting something?" Olive said from the front seat, her eyes on the figure on the porch.

Was that jealousy?

There was so much of him that wanted to say Cassie and he were a thing and she'd come to visit, but it wasn't true. Although, he figured he could probably get out of the car and pretend with Cassie and she would go along with it because while he didn't think that she actually had a thing for him, she did like him an awful lot. More than was suitable for a housekeeper. At least he'd always felt that way. Maybe she was just naturally flirty.

"No. That's Cassie, my housekeeper from Chicago. I had called and asked her to come up and fill the position here, but I never heard back from her. I didn't know she was going to be here."

That was the truth. Even though it wasn't what he wanted to say. He wanted to punish Olive just a little, maybe see if he could get her to feel some of the painful jealousy and hurt that he had felt, but it wasn't right.

"If you'd rather have her—"

"No. I would have brought her up here with me from Chicago to begin with if I wanted her, and I only contacted her out of desperation. I was afraid I was going to starve to death."

That might have been a bit of an exaggeration, but it made Olive snort just a little, and he appreciated that he could make her laugh, rather than make her jealous. If he loved her, truly loved her unselfishly the way God wanted him to, he wasn't going to try to hurt her every chance he got, no matter what she did to him. And he certainly wasn't going to go out of his way to make her jealous. In fact, he should go out of his way to keep her from being jealous. But that was if she was his.

Regardless, the command to treat others the way he wanted to be treated was first and foremost and it would be right for him to remember that.

"I'm probably going to have to give her a place to stay tonight. She doesn't have a car, either, and I won't be able to send her back to Chicago until tomorrow." He spoke as he looked at the sky which was on fire from the sunset. She could make it back to Chicago tonight, but he wasn't going to do that to her, as much as he didn't want her here and as annoyed as he was that she had shown up without saying anything. It was Cassie's personality to want to surprise him.

He got out of the car and went around like he usually did. Olive was out again, but he made it to the baby's door and was able to get the car seat out himself. She went to the back and started unloading groceries.

He grabbed several bags to carry in the hand that didn't have the car seat before they walked up to the porch together.

Cassie had gone from smiling in welcome to having her eyes narrowed, as though trying to figure out what was going on. The baby certainly would have thrown her off.

"I know you didn't have time to have a child since you left Chicago last year."

"Seems to me like it only takes nine months," he couldn't help but say. He shouldn't have been egging her on and continued to talk to try to make up for it. "But you're right. The baby isn't mine. But I have a housekeeper. I'm sorry you came all the way out here for nothing."

"You sent me a message and said you needed one."

"That was a month ago."

"A girl has to get her loose ends tied up."

"Maybe you could have answered my message and let me know that you were coming, and then I wouldn't have hired someone else."

"You hired a housekeeper that has a baby?" She sounded incredulous, if not annoyed. "That's foolish. I don't come with any such baggage, and I'm here now. So you can just tell her to go back where she came from."

"You can stay here for the night. But you have to make your own bed. And in the morning, I'll arrange for you to have a ride back to Chicago. I'm sorry you came the whole way out here for nothing." He ignored her suggestions, as he usually did. She was a bit more bossy than what he cared for, and he didn't particularly enjoy being told what to do. He didn't mind a discussion, even though he was technically the employer and she was the employee, but he was not going to take orders from his housekeeper.

Or ex-housekeeper as the case may be.

"I'm not going back. You can get rid of her. I have a long history with you, and you've been very happy with my services."

The way she said "services" sounded suggestive, and it made that icky chill that he often got around her clench around his backbone. It could have been his imagination, but beside him, Olive seemed to stiffen.

"I guess I'll let you guys hash this out. I'll go ahead and take these groceries in and start putting them away. If you need me to go, just tell me.... Can you carry the baby in?" she asked, since both of her hands were full.

"I'm coming in behind you." He could tell that there was a distance in her that hadn't been there before, or maybe more of a distance would be more accurate. Still, he wasn't trying to erase the distance between them. He had said himself he wanted to keep it there. So he didn't know why he was so upset about it.

Turning to Cassie, he reiterated his offer. "Come in, stay the night, but you're leaving in the morning. If you want to leave this evening, I am fine with that as well."

"I can't leave. I left everything in Chicago. I tied it all up, came here for you. Because you asked me to." Her words were snippy and annoyed. Like he had put her out somehow, when all he had done was ask her to fill a job, and when she hadn't responded, a month later, he hired someone else.

"It's not my fault you didn't correspond with me. How was I supposed to know that you were coming? Regardless, I will have someone take you back to Chicago in the morning."

"There's no place to go back to. What are you going to have them do? Dump me on the street?"

He stood there and stared at her. Was she serious?

But it didn't matter if she was, he couldn't have two women living under his roof.

Why not? He had the room. And it wasn't like he was short on money to pay them. The house didn't need a full-time housecleaner, and he certainly didn't need a full-time chef to make his meals, but that would make it easier on Olive, who already seemed like she wasn't healthy, with getting over malaria and childbirth. If she only had the cooking to do, and Cassie took care of the cleaning, he might actually be doing a favor to her.

He hadn't been looking for a way to do favors for Olive, but it did seem like she needed someone to take care of her. Cassie, on the other hand, could land on her feet. He didn't believe her about getting rid of all of her things in Chicago, and if she had, she should have the money behind her as a cushion to land somewhere. Plus, all of her family and friends were in Chicago. He felt like she would be fine.

"Come on in," he finally said, using one of his free fingers to open the door and hold it for Olive while she walked in ahead of him.

While he really did feel like he was making a decision that should make things easier for Olive, there was a bigger part of him that felt like it was flashing red warning lights indicating that this could be a very big, very bloody disaster.

Ten

"If you want your eggs made a different way, I'm happy to do it, but I recall your favorite was always scrambled with cheese."

Olive set the plate of eggs in front of Doyle who had settled himself down at the kitchen table at her request.

There was no sign of the other woman who had been there last night. Cassie. Olive had made a quick supper of chicken and veggies before she had stolen upstairs with her daughter.

Her stomach rumbled, but she hadn't talked to Doyle about whether she had to buy her own groceries or whether he provided her meals, and she didn't want to do that with Cassie hanging around trying to chat with him.

He didn't seem very talkative, and Olive didn't try to help the conversation along which died after each question Olive asked.

"These are fine. Whatever you make is fine. I'm not that picky. You know that."

She did. But she wanted to make him the food that he most enjoyed and wanted. Maybe he wanted a variety and didn't want to have to think about it.

"If it's okay with you, I'm going to go to Bible study this morning. I'll be back in time to put in a full eight hours, unless you wanted me to do more?" She was hoping not. Her recovery from malaria had been slow, probably complicated by the fact that the birth had been difficult and she lost a good bit of blood. It had just been a bad thing all the way around, and while she felt better than she did, she was still not up to her usual energy.

He paused, the fork halfway to his mouth.

"I thought you're going to sit down and eat with me." It wasn't a question, and it wasn't an invitation.

"We hadn't said, and I wasn't sure, and I didn't want to ask while Cassie was around last night." There, it wasn't that she didn't want to talk to him about it, she just felt like that would be more of a private conversation.

"I was thinking about hiring Cassie to do the housework while you could focus on the cooking." He looked down at his plate. "I thought that would be easier on you since it seems like malaria really did a number on you."

He'd noticed. That made her heart smile just a little, and it was absolutely true. But she didn't really want Cassie around. And she wasn't sure exactly why.

"It just seems like having two women in charge of the house is not a good idea. Unless you're willing to be very specific about whose domain is where. It...might lead to turf wars." She hoped that was enough humor to make it so that her comment didn't seem unkind. But she didn't think that she and Cassie would be able to get along. There was something about the way the woman looked at her that told her that she thought Doyle was hers, and she resented the fact that Olive was there.

"If you don't want her, I'll get rid of her today."

Really? He would do that for her? Or did he just not want fighting in the house? And she was the first one he had hired. Although, according to Cassie, she was the first one he had contacted.

"I'm going to be leaving in two months, and then you're going to be stuck trying to find another housekeeper, so maybe it would be better for you to have her, but if you're trying to make things easier on me, I'd rather do it all myself."

"I see. Well then, we'll try it for a week having both of you, with you cooking and her cleaning. Since you're going to be leaving, that will make things easier on me, and I do think it will make things easier on you, no matter what you say about turf wars."

Yeah. She'd been joking, but there'd been enough seriousness under it to show her concern.

"You're going to Bible study?" he asked, taking a sip of his water.

"Yes. Unless you have a problem with it. There is one every morning on Pastor Garnet's porch, and I feel like it's probably a good idea for me to go." She didn't say she needed it, but that's what she meant. She did. She needed it. She'd been away from the Lord too long, and she needed to get back. And Bible study was the best way to do it beyond reading her Bible and praying daily, which she had been doing.

"All right. I'll go with you."

She stopped, her mouth open. First, she'd said that she was going to take her car back and he said he'd go with her. Now he was going with her to Bible study?

But the idea that he might have been doing it for her slipped away with his next words. "I've been thinking about going, but I kept forgetting about it. Now that you've reminded me, I think I'll go today too."

She had turned to go back into the kitchen, so he didn't see her eyes wide open and her brows up to her hairline.

Okay. So it wasn't that she was shocked that he was a Christian, because she already knew that. Or that he was a strong Christian, because she knew that too. But the idea that he was voluntarily choosing to spend time with her was more than a little surprising. She figured that he hired her out of compassion and pity. And she also figured that he'd be avoiding her as much as he could. Yet here he was going to Bible study with her. He wasn't trying to avoid her.

"What time does it start?" He startled her, his voice coming from just above her shoulder.

She turned around, remembering again how tall he was and tilting her head. "Seven."

"I think we're supposed to take food."

"I don't think that's a prerequisite for being able to attend."

"It will take ten minutes to get there. Is there something you can make in half an hour?"

"I bought some blueberries for the salad that I was going to make later this week, but we could make a quick fruit salad."

"I'll forgo the blueberries in my salad later. But I just gave you more work to do. How about I do the dishes?"

"I thought the kitchen was my domain?" she asked softly, not wanting to push but knowing that confrontation was almost inevitable if Cassie was the kind of person she thought she was. The kind of person who pushed and pushed unless someone pushed back. Olive had never been very good at pushing back, she just left. She wasn't doing that anymore.

"Yes. The kitchen is yours. Unless you want her to clean it, and then I'll put that in her duties, but I'll make sure that she does it sometime when you're not in it. Perhaps an agreed-upon time?"

"That might be best." She didn't want to be accused of taking Cassie's mop and bucket and cleaning supplies, and she could hardly ask for Doyle to buy her supplies of her own.

It just complicated everything, but she couldn't blame him for hiring her, because he'd been waiting a month for a housekeeper, and he finally had one drop on his doorstep, but she was going to be leaving soon. The smartest thing for him to have done would have been to get rid of her.

Plus, maybe she had judged Cassie wrong, and she wasn't going to have the issues with her that she thought she was. Yeah. She should have given her the benefit of the doubt instead of immediately imagining that they were going to have all kinds of trouble. That wasn't right of her.

"I'm going to have to change Livvy before we go," she said as she finished putting the fruit salad together and clamped the lid down tight.

He had put the dishes in the dishwasher and wiped the table. He was now rinsing out the rag he'd used and laying it carefully out on the counter so it would dry.

"That's fine. I'll text Cassie and see if she wants to go too, but I'm guessing she's probably not up yet. That was one of the struggles that I had when she worked for me before. I was on my own for breakfast."

He didn't seem like he was complaining, just stating a fact as he pulled his phone up and began to text.

She'd forgotten how easy it was to be with him. He worked hard. It was hard for her to think of anyone who worked harder, but he didn't have the frenetic pace that a lot of hardworking men had, where they didn't have time for anything but to go directly from task to task and never have time to stop or chat or want to discuss anything but what was on their mind.

He was always willing to take the time to talk to her. Had always been interested in things outside of his little bubble. In fact, the conversations she had with Doyle had been the best conversations she'd had in her life and so much different than living with her parents, who hadn't wanted to have much to do with her. It was convenient how she had forgotten all of those things. Or maybe pushed them aside.

She couldn't believe she had given him up because of some misguided idea of needing to travel the world. Even before she'd gotten sick, she wasn't having that much fun. It was enjoyable, and she loved seeing new things, but it was enjoyable the way eating a candy bar was enjoyable. Empty calories.

"If she answers me, I'll let you know. In the meantime, we'll just plan on going without her."

She nodded as she knelt down by where she had set Livvy on a blanket on the floor. She had been happy and content cooing and gurgling by herself.

"Who watched her while you were sick?" Doyle asked as though the thought had just occurred to him.

"I don't know. I was unconscious, delirious at times, and too weak to move most of the time. Sometimes I would look over and she would be in a crib in my room, and sometimes she wouldn't be. A couple of times, I got out of bed to find her, and once I fell down on the floor, cracked my head, and ended up unconscious for I don't know how long. I don't remember who got me back in the bed. It was...not a good time."

To say the least. She didn't know how Livvy had even survived. But the neglect had made her into a very content baby. Perhaps because she had learned that crying didn't bring her any attention so it was a pointless and fruitless endeavor. The idea was sad, but it made for an easy baby anyway. She couldn't go back and change it though. She couldn't continue to feel guilty for things that she couldn't undo.

Like leaving Doyle.

"I'm sorry I hurt you," she said as she carefully closed the tabs of the diaper and started to put her outfit back together.

She hadn't planned to apologize, but it felt good.

"I don't think about it."

Of course he didn't. It probably didn't bother him at all.

"I just know I didn't treat you very well, and that's weighed on my mind since I left. It's weighed even harder on it since I've come back. You've been so nice to me, and I don't deserve it. I just wanted you to know that I'm sorry. I would do it differently if I could go back and do it again, but since I can't, I'll just try not to do anything like that to anyone again."

"Yeah. That's probably a good idea going forward."

There might have been a little bit of irony or perhaps humor in his voice, but she didn't turn around to check. She snapped the last of Livvy's snaps and lifted her from the floor, carefully picking up the blanket and shaking it out before she wrapped it around her.

It wasn't long until she had her tucked in the car seat, and she didn't need to say anything because as soon as the baby was ready, Doyle picked her up in one hand, held the fruit salad and the spoon in the other, and led the way to the door.

She slipped around him, opening it for them, while he walked out.

"Do you want me to lock it?" she asked, knowing that growing up she couldn't recall her parents ever locking the door, but times had changed, and perhaps Doyle's time in Chicago had changed him.

"Yeah. You better. Cassie's up there, and I wouldn't want her to get any unexpected visitors. Otherwise, I typically don't."

"I thought after living in Chicago..." She allowed her voice to trail off, thinking that he could elaborate on that if he wanted to.

"Yeah. I wouldn't leave my door unlocked there. It took a little while to transition back to a small town, but it's nice to not have to worry about whether or not someone unsavory is going to be getting in. Here in Raspberry Ridge, that's almost unheard of."

"One of the reasons why I wanted to come back and raise my child here."

"I think that was a smart decision."

They got in the car and drove to Bible study without saying anything more. Unlike yesterday though, this silence was not uncomfortable. It didn't seem as peaceful and natural as the silences she remembered from before, but maybe they were starting to get used to each other.

Eleven

There were cars on both sides of the road in front of Pastor Garnet's house as they pulled out on the street. Doyle didn't want Olive to have to walk so far, but he was sure if he let her out, she wasn't going to leave without the baby at least, which would defeat the purpose of him helping her. So he parked his car as close as he could.

"This seems like a popular destination."

"Well, there's not much going on in small towns, but I've heard really good things about the Bible study, and I know Pastor Garnet does an excellent job."

"Perhaps because he's your future brother-in-law, you have a bias?" Doyle glanced over at her, and she looked a little sheepish.

"Perhaps."

He was teasing her, and she knew it, and something had gone through the air between them that was more than words. He loved that little bit of communication without having to say anything at all. He felt that with other people at times, but there was just something about Olive that made him feel like she actually knew him, or cared about him, or something. She did it again today when she had made the eggs the way she knew he liked them. It had been years since she had cooked for him, and even then, she hadn't done it much. They'd never lived together. But maybe she just noticed the way he'd ordered them when they'd gone out. Whatever it was, however she did it, she took the time to remember, and he appreciated that. It made him feel like she cared.

And he shouldn't do that. That way lay hurt. At least that was what his brain was trying to say.

They walked up on the porch, with him carrying the baby and her carrying the fruit salad.

"Olive! I'm so glad you could make it," Mertie said, coming over and giving her sister a hug. "It was so kind of you to bring her," Mertie murmured to him, and he almost thought that perhaps she was seeing the same thing he was, that Olive wasn't well.

"Glad you can make it," Dominic said, coming over to shake his hand. Dominic was a deacon at the church and had been instrumental in getting Pastor Garnet to come.

"Where's your wife? And your six kids?" Doyle couldn't help but add that last part, along with the number. He knew that Dominic couldn't really believe that he actually had six children. After years of his wife and him thinking that they weren't going to have any more after their only son died, God had abundantly blessed them.

"One of the kids is sick, and we didn't want to bring him to potentially spread it to everyone else. I was going to stay home and let Vera come, but she insisted." He held up his hands like he had nothing to do with it. "Far be it for me to argue with a sleep-deprived mom of twins."

"I'll take your word on that, hopefully never learning from experience," Doyle said, only half joking. He did want to have children someday. A few, not just one, but preferably one at a time.

He watched as Olive chatted with a few other ladies and then made her way to the step where she sat down with the car seat sitting on the porch beside and a little bit behind her.

Livvy had fallen asleep, and he assumed that she was probably going to stay that way throughout the entire study.

He wanted to go over and sit down beside her, hold her hand, even sit behind her and cradle her between his legs, but they didn't have that kind of relationship.

Not anymore.

"All right, I think all the food is here, so we're able to get started," Pastor Garnet said, amid the laughter of everyone. Then they quieted down, and he continued. "Let's pray first."

He said a short prayer for the food and for the lesson while the porch was silent other than the soft breeze that blew over everyone.

"Amen. You all can grab something to eat if you haven't. I'm gonna say a few words while you do so." Most everyone had gotten food, but there were a few who stood at his invitation while he continued to talk. "We're out of Deuteronomy, and we're starting Joshua today. I read this earlier and couldn't help but smile, because it contains one of my favorite verses. Joshua 1:8. 'This book of the law shall not depart out of thy mouth; but thou shalt meditate therein day and night, that thou may observe to do according to all that is written therein...'"

He put a hand on his Bible. "We'll read the entire chapter here in a minute, but I just wanted to talk about that verse for a moment, because I think it's one of the most important verses in the Bible. There is a premise at the end, and if you are following along in your Bible, you could see that I didn't read it. But God promises that if Joshua does what He commands, He will make his way prosperous and he will have good success. He's talking about conquering Canaan. That's where his way will be prosperous and he will have good success."

He paused for a moment as though gathering his thoughts. "In the Bible, Canaan represents the promised land, of course, but the part that needs to be conquered represents sin. There were people there doing all kinds of wicked things, things that we in our modern sensitivities can barely even imagine. We think we're so new and progressive by encouraging sodomy and promiscuity and lasciviousness, but trust me, it was all going on back then as well. We're not as suave and sophisticated as we like to believe."

He shook his head. "But that's not really what I wanted to say. I wanted to point out that God gives a recipe for success. A recipe for being able to conquer sin. Being able to eradicate it and get it out of your life. That's what they were going to do with the people who inhabited Canaan. They were going to eradicate them and get them completely out."

He paused for a moment, as though thinking about how he was going to phrase this next bit, and then he spoke. "Right there, that verse, it says that we should meditate on God's word day and night. It should be in our mouth continually. I think this Bible study is good, and I can't take credit for starting it, so don't think that I am. But when Homer and Skyler decided to read the Bible through and to do a little bit every day, I think they were on the exact right path that a person needs to do in order to eradicate sin from their life." He held his Bible up and waved it carefully. "This book is powerful. It's God's word. How could it not be? And how could we not infuse that power into our very souls if we read it, think about it, and try to understand it on a daily basis?"

He put the Bible back in his lap as everyone sat quietly, the lake breeze blowing over them, ruffling a few pages, allowing hair and clothes to blow, warming in the morning summer sun.

"So often we think we're too busy. We think we don't have time. We think we'll catch up tomorrow, or we'll do it later, and then a few days slip into a week, and before we know it, it's been months or years since we opened our Bible. And things that we used to think were wrong don't seem so wrong anymore. That's the way sin is. I don't know about you, but when I look in the Bible, and I see God talk about sin, I think the devil is going to show up with his pitchfork and his horns and I'm going to be able to see that sin, and I'm going to take a big stand against it," he said, using his voice's inflection to emphasize his words. "But sin isn't like that. It's just a little bit, just little, often deceptive, and happens on a day-by-day basis. We make a decision to do something we want to do, and we don't know or don't care the Bible tells us it's wrong. That decision leads to another decision, and that decision doesn't seem wrong either. I don't think our country would be in the state that it was in if we hadn't left off reading our Bibles on a daily basis, teaching it in school, and staying away from sin."

He paused for a moment, and then he said, "I don't want to get political, but I don't think abortion is a political issue. I think it's a moral one. A lot of the things that we think of as political issues are moral issues. Sodomy for example. That's not a political issue. It's a moral issue. God clearly denounces it and commands us to do so as well.

It's the same for abortion. The ten commandments say thou shall not kill. In the Psalms, David said you formed me in my mother's womb. Obviously God was forming him in his womb before he was born. When is a baby a human? I don't know. I'm not a scientist, although it doesn't seem to matter what science says anymore. Regardless, whether a baby has a soul at conception, or whether it's a week before they're born, do you want to mess up and accidentally kill a human being? Do you want to take that chance?"

He took a breath.

"I'm going to get off my soapbox, but I think the more we're in this book, the more we understand how the world is, and how they try to justify what they do, and it sounds okay. But as for me, I will never, ever vote for anyone who thinks abortion is okay. I do not want to be complicit in that sin. I don't care what the rest of their agenda is, I will sit out an election before I cast a single vote that might allow a baby to die on my watch. And I'm fighting to make sure my tax dollars aren't being used to fund a procedure that I feel is murder. That God says is murder."

He seemed to deflate a little. "I'm sorry, I get a little fired up about sin. That's just an example of how we leave the Bible and start to think that sin isn't that bad. That we can vote for someone who murders babies and it's okay. But the idea is God wants us to be in the Bible every day. And we think other things are more important. They aren't. There is nothing more important than being in your Bible on a daily basis, yourself. With others if you want, but every day. You should be there. And if you are, God promises that you will prosper and have good success against sin. It's not talking about monetary success, which may or may not happen. It's talking about success against sin. Against the forces that would try to take you out of the battle for good and right. Because, folks, there is a battle."

He opened his Bible. "All right, let's start reading from verse one. As always, read as much as you feel comfortable with, and if you don't want to read, just motion to the person beside you, and they'll pick up. And don't worry about butchering the words, because I butcher them too." He grinned, and everyone laughed.

They started reading, and Doyle was surprised at how much he had enjoyed the study by the time they were done. Pastor Garnet didn't drag it out, but he did give some pertinent information and gave him some things to think about. It was interesting to read the Bible, to have some new things pointed out, and to see the old familiar words that hadn't changed over his lifetime. And it was especially good to remember how important it was to stay in the Book, since evil was all around them.

"All right, folks. That's it for today. But Mertie, Dabney, and I do have an announcement." He paused while the ladies he had named came up and stood on either side of him, and he put an arm around both of them and drew them near.

"Mertie and I are going to get married, and we're going to do that this Friday afternoon at the personal care center where Pastor Calvin and his wife live. They're going to perform the ceremony. Weather permitting, it's going to be outside. If not, we have permission to use their auditorium. You all are invited. If you bring food, we'll eat. If you don't, we won't, but I felt like it was important to have Pastor Calvin there, since he and his wife had so much influence on Mertie's and Dabney's and my lives."

Applause rang out, and happy congratulations rang in the air.

"And then the week after that, he's going to marry us." Hobert stood up with his arm around Amara. Doyle wasn't sure that any woman could smile any bigger than what she was as she looked around the group and then glanced lovingly up at her husband-to-be. "That's going to happen at the church, and everyone here is invited. It's not going to be formal, and the same rules about food apply." Hobert grinned, and everyone laughed.

Two weddings after so many years of not even one. That was great for the town of Raspberry Ridge, but it made Doyle reflect on his life, thinking that if he would have had his way, Olive and he would be celebrating eight or ten years of married life.

He knew that most people would say that they had been too young to get married, but he felt like it wasn't really about age, it was more about beliefs and commitment.

It didn't matter though. Those years were past, and he wasn't any closer to getting married now than he had been in the years since.

"If it's okay with you, I'd really like to go to both of those weddings. They're my sisters. I know I just started—"

"You'd already asked for Friday. The two of us can go together, since I was going to take you to take your car back. And then, we'll just plan on doing it again next Friday, only not driving so far."

He wanted to do more with her, wanted to spend time with her, wanted to get to know her again, but he needed to stop pushing. That was all well and good, after he just insisted they were going to spend the next two Fridays together.

"How are things going with the twins, Dominic?" Hobert asked as Doyle and Olive stood up to leave.

He listened to Dominic talk about how difficult it was to have six children and how much fun it had been as well. It seemed like their house was bursting with life and love and happiness, and he'd never seen his wife Vera look better. He did say something about the grocery bill killing him.

"Are you ready?" Doyle said softly to Olive as she picked up the car seat. Livvy hadn't stirred.

He wanted to get her out of there though, because she looked exhausted. White as a sheet and she seemed to be trembling, although it could have been his imagination.

"Here, I'll carry her," he said after she nodded at him. "I'm going to grab the fruit salad bowl too. It looked to me like it was empty when I went up to get a drink just before we started."

She nodded. The fact that she looked terrible and she didn't give him any grief about carrying the baby concerned him.

He needed to look up malaria and see exactly how long it was supposed to be before a person got over it. Or maybe it was just the fact that she had been sick and her body needed to rest and recover, but instead she had been traveling the world and taking care of her little one and worried because she had no money and no job.

They walked to the car in silence, and he tried hard to resist the urge to put his arm around her and tell her to lean on him.

Instead, after they had gotten in the car and started toward home, he said, "I think it might be a good idea for you to lie down when we get home. You look tired, and you've been through a lot the last few months."

"I'm fine. I'll feel a lot better once we get out and I can stretch my legs some."

He didn't know how that had anything to do with anything, but he didn't argue with her. As he pulled into the drive, it was almost déjà vu all over again. Since Cassie was standing on the porch and seemed like she was waiting for them.

Olive stiffened, there was no doubt about it, but she didn't say anything. She silently got out, and for the first time, she beat him to the back door and unhooked the car seat herself.

He was waiting as she backed out of the door, and he closed it before taking the car seat from her.

He put his hand on it, and she met his gaze and held it for several seconds.

She didn't say anything, and he didn't either. Was she going to allow him to carry it? Or was she going to demand that she did?

Finally, after several long moments, she pulled her hand away. Her face seemed to have some kind of pasty sweat breaking out on it, and he wanted to insist again that she go lie down.

"I have lunch in the oven. It'll be ready right at noon. And I made a list of all the groceries that I'm going to need, and if you don't mind, I'm going to borrow your car and get them right now. That way, I'll be home in plenty of time to cook supper." Cassie spoke from the porch where she waved her phone around. He assumed that that meant the list was on it.

"When we talked, I said you would do the cleaning and Olive would do the cooking. That's if you stay."

"I'm staying. And I have the cooking under control, so Olive doesn't need to." She lifted her shoulder and then stepped down off the porch. "Just keep an eye on the oven. I have it turned down low, and there shouldn't be any problems, but just in case I get held up in town, don't forget about it."

He wasn't sure what to say. He wanted to tell her that he didn't need her at all, but seeing how terrible Olive looked, he knew she couldn't handle any cleaning, and he wasn't quite sure whether she would be able to handle the cooking either.

Instead, when Cassie came over to him and held her hand out for his keys, perhaps against his better judgment, he dug them out of his pocket and set them in her hand.

"I can either pay for them myself, or you can give me your credit card. It's up to you. I'll give you a bill later."

"You can bill me later, but Olive and I already went shopping for the next three days, and we're covered. There isn't any need for you to go."

"There are some things in the kitchen I need but don't have. I guess she doesn't know what staples you should stock the kitchen with."

"I hadn't known what the kitchen had when I went shopping." It was the first Olive had spoken since Bible study, and he winced at how weak her voice sounded. Maybe the morning with cooking and caring for the baby and then going to Bible study was just too much.

"She's right. I asked her to cook for me and took her shopping before she even saw my kitchen. So, you can keep the slams to yourself." He paused for a moment, and then, remembering what Olive had said the night before and hoping to head some of that off, he continued, "I'll let you stay. You can clean, and you can cook when Olive is not up to it, because she's recovering from having a baby and from being sick. But if you're going to have little underhanded insults and constantly try to undermine her position here, you're going to go." He didn't like to be unkind, and he didn't want to be mean, but at the same time, he wasn't going to accept Cassie's insults and complaints.

That was not going to make a very harmonious household, and Olive didn't have the strength to defend herself.

"I didn't mean anything by it. It's just if you guys already went shopping, there's more things that need to be bought." She didn't apologize, and she didn't look the slightest bit upset, just defensive.

Part of him said that he probably should get rid of her now, part of him wanted to give her the benefit of the doubt. It's what he would want done for him. Maybe she was just afraid that she wasn't going to get the job and she felt like she needed to show how she was superior to her competition.

"Come on, let's go." He spoke to Olive, and that time, he really did put his arm around her, and either she was okay with it or she was too tired or weak to fight him, because she didn't try to shrug it off but instead allowed him to help her balance as they walked up the stairs. He set the car seat down in order for him to open the door.

"Maybe I will go ahead and lie down for a little bit if that's okay. She did say she had lunch in the oven." Olive's voice came out just barely above a whisper as he closed the door and set the car seat down.

"Do you mind carrying her to my room?" She didn't say she was too weak to do that, she just asked for a favor.

"How about I leave her out here with me? If she wakes up, tell me what to do."

She paused, her eyes half closed and downcast as she seemed to consider his request.

"Are you sure you don't mind?" she said, and when he shook his head, she gave him the instructions to make the bottle of formula, telling him how much Livvy usually drank.

"Be sure to burp her. She's burping some on her own, but if you don't, she'll get a bellyache."

"Got it. Bellyache bad. Burping good."

She huffed out a breath, although her smile was so faint he almost missed it. "I'm sorry. I thought I was going to bounce back a little faster than what I have. The last few days have been pretty jam-packed full, and I think it's just caught up with me."

"Go take a rest. I'll watch Livvy, and you need to sleep."

"You're probably better off hiring Cassie. She doesn't have to sleep in the middle of the day. Wait. It's not the middle of the day. I haven't even made it to lunchtime yet."

"It's okay. This is just a little bit of someone taking care of you in order for you to get better. How can you expect to do that when you have to do everything yourself?"

She looked at him, almost as though she were trying to understand what he said and formulate an answer.

"Go to bed. You can argue with me when you get up."

At this point, he almost welcomed her arguments, just to show that she was feeling okay.

He watched her walk away, seeing that she opened the door he assigned to her last night as her bedroom and disappeared inside.

He looked down at the baby, sleeping soundly in the car seat. He had never taken care of a baby before. And now, he had volunteered to take care of this one. What had he been thinking?

Well, if he had any questions, he knew how to use the internet, and he supposed he could probably find the answers. For now, he wasn't going to borrow trouble. She was sleeping, and he hoped she stayed that way. If not, he would deal with it.

Twelve

Olive woke suddenly, seeming to come up from a deep, dark place and wondering immediately where in the world she was.

She blinked at her unfamiliar surroundings, trying to remember what country she was in. And what year it was.

It looked like the sun was going down, like maybe it was late afternoon, but where?

Then, as she lay there, things started to come back to her, and immediately she thrust the blankets off and jumped out of bed.

She felt a little dizzy for a second and put a hand out on the nightstand to steady herself before she hurried to the door.

She was at Doyle's house. He was watching her baby. She was supposed to be his housekeeper, but she went to bed right after they got home from Bible study this morning and... She pulled out her phone which was still in her pocket and looked at the time.

Yeah, almost four. Had she really slept that long? And hadn't heard a thing.

What about Livvy?

With that thought, she pulled the door open and hurried out into the hall.

The living room came into view almost immediately, and her steps slowed. Doyle sat on the couch, Livvy cradled in one arm. With the other hand, he fed her, while one of her hands touched the bottle and one of them gripped his finger.

He had a phone pressed between his ear and his shoulder, and he was talking softly on it.

It looked like he had everything under complete control.

She put a hand up to her chest where her heart beat hard. It was okay; she could calm down. Although, this was just one more thing that she owed Doyle for. Being kind to her baby, taking care of her when she needed a break.

She felt like every second she stayed here, she owed him more and more. But he didn't act like she owed him. He acted like he was just doing what was normal.

Something smelled really good, and she heard some pots clanging in the kitchen. Maybe she'd lost her job after all. Maybe he was going to kick her out. Of course, she wasn't leaving without her baby. But something told her that Doyle wasn't going to do that. He came to her defense rather quickly when Cassie had tried to shove her aside earlier, and he made sure he encouraged her to get the rest she needed. Like he really did want her to recover and not overdo it.

In fact, she really couldn't think of a single thing that he'd done that hadn't been with her in mind.

In the meantime, she felt like she'd done nothing but mooch off of him. She hadn't even done the cooking that she had been hired to do.

"Are you finally awake?" he said, and she realized she'd gone to the opening of the living room and just stood there, and in the meantime, he'd gotten off the phone.

"I can't believe I slept so long. I'm so sorry. I didn't mean to leave you with Livvy for such a long time."

"We've been fine. You didn't have to rush out of bed to come check the second you woke up."

How did he—she put a hand up to her hair. Yeah. She probably looked ridiculous with her hair sticking up all over the place and her clothes all rumpled.

"You can go back, take care of yourself, take your time. You can see we're good."

"Yes. Thank you."

"And you're going to sit down beside me and eat. I have a feeling you didn't eat any of the two meals that you cooked for me."

He was right. She hadn't eaten. "We didn't really talk about that, and I didn't want to steal food."

"You're not stealing food. Your meals are included with your employment. And I will consider it a breach of contract if you don't eat."

She didn't think he was actually serious about the breach of contract thing, but the idea that he was going to make sure that she ate was a relief.

"I'm starving." She still felt a little dizzy, and that was most likely because he was right. She really hadn't eaten other than a couple bits of fruit at Bible study.

"Good. You get yourself ready, and as soon as Livvy is done with her bottle, I'll walk into the kitchen and see what's going on for supper."

"You don't have to eat early because of me."

"Maybe I'll get some leftovers from lunch. We'll figure something out, just take care of yourself, okay?"

She nodded, wishing that she was able to have the strength that she wanted in order to take care of him. That was the way it was supposed to be, not him taking care of her.

But she supposed sometimes God gave people trials to go through so that other people could learn to take care of them. At least she'd heard that from somewhere. Maybe while she was sick in Ecuador, she heard a missionary saying that. That sometimes people were laid up just so the people around them could learn to be servants.

She didn't really want to be the reason that someone else learned to serve, but it seemed to be a necessary part of God's plan.

She walked slowly back to her room, feeling better after her rest but knowing that some food in her belly would make her feel even better and very, very grateful that Doyle was insisting on it.

After washing her face, brushing her hair and her teeth, and taking care of other necessities, as well as changing her clothes, she felt almost decent again, though still a little weak and wobbly. She was very thirsty, but at least she wasn't exhausted anymore.

When she walked back out to the living room, Doyle was no longer there, so she went straight through and found him in the kitchen.

"I was just getting some things ready," Doyle said.

"Smells like Cassie has made something delicious," Olive said, wanting to give credit where it was due, even if it did eventually get her fired.

"Cassie is a really good cook," Doyle said, his brows furrowed as though he were looking her over and trying to make sure that she was okay. "How about you go and sit down at the table? I'm almost done putting this together."

"It would have been better if we let it cook a little bit longer. But I started these poor carrots earlier than I should have, and they happen to be ready."

"I love carrots. That sounds delicious." She really wanted to be friends with Cassie. If they could. She just didn't want Cassie to be able to push her around.

"Go on. Go sit." Doyle wasn't commanding her, necessarily, although he did take the hand that wasn't holding the baby and make a shooing motion with it.

"I know when I'm not wanted," she said as she left, joking mostly, although there was something about seeing him in the kitchen with Cassie that...didn't sit right with her. She had no reason for it not to. Doyle was not hers; she had rejected him when he had wanted them to be more. She had no leg to stand on.

She also didn't have the strength to argue. So she walked slowly into the dining room and sat down, making sure she didn't use the chair that Doyle had been in earlier that day, just in case that was his chair.

The house was nice, if in need of a few updates. There was some paint peeling on the walls and a few spots on the ceiling. The carpet was old and ragged, and if it was her, she would yank it up and put tile or hardwood down. Something warmer yet easy to clean. Something a little more modern but not so modern that it made the house feel out of place.

She didn't have long to wait, and what felt like just a few seconds later, Doyle came in carrying a plate he piled high with mashed potatoes and gravy and chicken, and some carrots on the side.

"I thought she said she wasn't planning on having a meal this early and it wasn't ready?"

"We figured it out. I thought it was important for you to eat."

He started to pull out a chair, one that was catty-corner from her, so he was sitting at the end of the table and she was sitting beside him on his left.

"Aren't you going to eat?"

"I just ate lunch not that long ago. But I was going to sit with you while you did, if that's okay." He carefully sat down, holding the baby with confidence but also moving a little more gingerly than he normally might. He always had a grace about him, but he seemed to be extra cautious while Livvy was in his arms.

"I hope she didn't give you any trouble," Olive said after she had said a silent prayer to herself. Thanking God for the food and for the place of refuge, because that's what this felt like. A place where she could lay her burdens down and where she was among friends.

"Not a second of trouble. She fussed a little when she woke up. I checked her diaper and fed her. And that made her happy. And then she wasn't hungry until the last bottle that you saw me giving her, so that's two while you were sleeping, in case you need to keep track."

He looked a little uncertain, and it made her want to smile. But it was cute, and she didn't want to make him feel like he hadn't done a good job.

"I don't need to keep track, but I appreciate you thinking that I might and doing it for me. It sounds to me like you've done an excellent job. Are you sure you don't have any experience with babies?" she asked, putting a bite of mashed potatoes in her mouth and almost closing her eyes with how good it felt to be eating again.

"I have a couple hours of experience under my belt now. I suppose I could be a nanny. Do you know anyone who's hiring?" he asked, and there was no mistaking the humor lurking in his eyes.

That made her a little bit jealous. Maybe he and Cassie had been out here having a good time while she was sleeping and that was why he was in such a good mood.

But her brain tried to shut that down right away. He had been sitting on the couch, feeding the baby, and talking on the phone when she got up. Cassie had been nowhere in sight. It wasn't like they were having a free-for-all out here. And if they were, it was none of her business.

"I don't, but I'll definitely keep your name in my Rolodex in case I come upon someone who is in the market for an exceptionally good nanny."

There, her teasing tone matched his, and there was none of the seriousness that she felt in her heart.

Lord, I don't want to worry about tomorrow. You've taken care of today so beautifully, why would I think that You wouldn't do the same for me tomorrow? Help me to trust in You, and please, help me not to be filled with regret over the past or jealousy over Doyle. Help me to love him the way You want me to and to be happy if he's found happiness with someone else. That's how I'm supposed to feel.

"You went quiet," Doyle said as he shifted Livvy in his arms, holding her against his chest so that she could look out.

"I'm sorry. I guess I'm so used to being alone that I forgot that I'm supposed to be keeping up my end of the conversation. Where's Cassie? Doesn't she want to eat with us?"

"She's on the clock. And she ate when I did."

She jerked her head up and put a bite of the carrot in her mouth. She had to admit, Cassie really knew how to cook. And if they ate together, so what? He was sitting with her now.

"These are the best carrots I've ever eaten," she said, meaning every word.

"They were okay," Doyle said with a lift of his shoulder. Like it wasn't that big of a deal.

But it was, because Cassie was the one who was supposed to be cleaning, and instead she was doing Olive's job. Because Olive couldn't. Because Olive was sleeping. She hadn't even taken care of her baby.

"Should I plan on cleaning the house, if Cassie is going to do the cooking?"

"No. This was just for today, relax. You needed some extra sleep, you got it. Now you're getting some nourishment, and tomorrow you're going to feel a lot better. You can pick up where you left off tomorrow morning for breakfast. After all, Cassie is not getting up for breakfast."

"Maybe I should do the cooking and cleaning before noon, and she should do the cooking and cleaning in the afternoon."

She didn't really mean that as a legitimate suggestion, she was just poking fun at her penchant for getting up early and Cassie's tendency to want to sleep in.

"You know what, that sounds like a really good compromise. You could be off by twelve, and she could be off by six. If I eat at five, that would give her an hour to do the dishes afterward." He nodded his head. "I'll run it by her, but I'm pretty sure that's what we'll do. Unless she has a major problem with that."

There might be a major problem. One of them might like to keep the sugar on the counter, while the other one wanted to keep it in the cupboard. She could see something along those lines being a potential for arguments, but as long as she just gave in and allowed Cassie to keep things wherever she wanted to, they would probably get along just fine.

That wasn't her being a doormat, that was her giving up her way in order to foster harmony in the home. If it were a moral issue, it would be wrong for her to just give in or give up, but since it wasn't, it was better for her to give up her way for the sake of getting along. That was dying to self for the sake of Jesus.

Hopefully that was all it was going to take for things to go smoothly, but somehow she doubted it.

Thirteen

Maybe she really liked this new schedule after all, Olive thought to herself as she strolled down the drive a few days later. It was Thursday, and her sister was getting married the next day.

She'd talked to them the day before, and they were planning on doing some work this afternoon on the house. Since she'd been here, she hadn't given them a hand at all.

Amara had told her not to worry about it, that they all understood that she had had a baby and she'd been sick on top of that. Still, she wanted to pull her weight and not dump everything on her sisters. That was the old her. The new her was trying to turn a new leaf over. For some reason, that leaf seemed awfully heavy.

Regardless, it was a beautiful summer day along the shores of Lake Michigan, with the lake breeze blowing through her hair and rippling the grasses along either side of the driveway. Livvy, content in her car seat, was wide-awake, with her big brown eyes looking everywhere, as though she were actually taking it all in. She seemed so wise. Olive could only hope that she would grow up to be as wise as she seemed, a lot wiser than her mother at least.

Wiser than her father, who'd gotten involved with someone aside from his wife.

Olive would never have been with him if she had realized he was married, but she shouldn't have been intimate with someone she wasn't married to anyway, so she knew the fault for that lay on her shoulders.

She shoved all those thoughts aside. That was her past. That was the person she was before she rededicated her life to Christ. She didn't expect an overnight change, although she did understand that sometimes Jesus did change people that quickly and easily. He hadn't done that for her, but he'd given her the desire, not necessarily the will.

That was fine. She would grow in character every time she didn't allow her flesh to win.

She hadn't realized how long it was from Doyle's house to their mansion, and she was exhausted by the time she climbed her driveway. There weren't many hills in Michigan, but that one seemed particularly steep and she was panting by the time she was up to the top, having had to stop three times and set the car seat down.

Finally, standing at the door, she wasn't sure whether she should knock or not. It was her house too, but she didn't want to walk in on anything since both of her sisters were engaged to be married.

And neither one of them would be doing anything inappropriate. She was sure of it.

So, rather than raising her hand to knock, she put her hand on the knob and opened the door.

Mertie and Garnet jerked apart as they heard the door open.

They were fully dressed, embracing in the kitchen, but it was a little bit awkward.

"I'm sorry. I did debate about whether or not I should knock."

Mertie's cheeks had flooded with color. She didn't very often see her sister flustered, and she almost wanted to stand there and enjoy it. If she hadn't been so tired, she would have.

"Oh. It's okay. We were just..."

"You don't have to explain," Olive broke in, not wanting to hear whatever Mertie was going to say they were doing.

"I think I forgot to call you. In fact, I know I did." She grimaced, glanced at Garnet, and then looked back to Olive.

"About what?" Olive asked, realizing that Amara was nowhere to be seen.

"This morning, Dominic called Garnet and asked if he would be able to go to the ladies' Bible study that his wife usually leads for a neighbor down the road. You probably don't know her, since she and her husband just moved to Raspberry Ridge not that long ago. Her name is Norma Jean. And her husband is Miles. They are...struggling a little in their marriage, and Vera has been working with them, but since she's had the twins, she's not been able to make it out as much as she's wanted to."

"While Mertie talked to Norma Jean, I've been talking with Miles. He definitely loves his wife and wants to be a better husband." Garnet paused. "If you'd like, you can come along. She has a daughter, Holly, and while Livvy is way too young to play with Holly, Holly would still probably enjoy seeing her."

"Of course. And it would be good for Livvy to get out and see new people." The idea of walking all that way made her want to lie down on the floor.

Maybe Mertie saw that because she said, "It's a beautiful day, but I think we ought to drive. I bet that car seat gets heavy if you try carrying it for any type of distance."

"I'm glad you said that. I thought I was a weakling because I had to stop three times on the way up the driveway and take a rest. It is heavy."

"We'll drive. If you're sure you don't mind going. I'm sorry I didn't call. Amara was there when I got the message, and she decided she would go out on the boat with Hobert today. So... I don't want to see you working by yourself, and we almost have it ready to go."

"I'd love to go along." The idea of working was almost beyond her, but she also was curious as to what kind of ladies' Bible study Mertie might be doing. She was reading the Bible on her own, but so many times, she couldn't make a whole lot out of it.

And a few of the Bible studies she looked up online didn't really follow the Bible. They seemed to have more of a social or political bent than actual truth. And she knew that whatever Mertie's faults might be, Mertie wasn't going to take the Bible and change it into anything other than what it actually said and then apply it to everyday living. She listened to Mertie a few times online, and she'd always been impressed with her sister's wisdom. She supposed that came from reading the

Bible a lot, but she hardly hoped to aspire to ever be half that wise herself.

But maybe hanging around wise people was another way, other than reading the Bible, for her to do that.

Garnet's phone rang, and he glanced at the number. Then, he gave an apologetic glance to Mertie before he said, "I better take this."

Mertie nodded, and she stayed in the kitchen while he walked into the living room and answered the phone.

"I'm sorry. He's been having some issues all day with a family down the road whose oldest son is trying to run away. He's been counseling them, and they are understandably devastated. He's been trying to work things out, but... It's a sad situation." Mertie pressed her lips together and then said, "Can I get you some tea?"

"I can get myself a glass of water. Garnet hasn't even been the pastor a week yet. I can't believe he is having to deal with something like that."

"It's always something, all the time. And I guess I knew this, because I've been in the ministry and I've seen it at different churches that I've gone to, but the congregation just really doesn't understand everything that a pastor goes through."

"And they probably don't give the pastor's wife any credit either, since your plans get interrupted, again and again."

"I suppose that's true. I wondered before I accepted his proposal whether I would be able to handle it. I know there are going to be times where I'm going to feel neglected because it's going to feel like he puts his congregation ahead of me."

"But he's doing a good work. Working for the Lord."

"I know. I think sometimes no matter how many good things our husbands do, we still want them to pay attention to us. Right?"

That was the kind of wisdom Olive had been thinking about. Mertie wasn't even married yet, and she already knew that there were going to be times where she was going to have to fight those feelings.

"How did you get to be so wise?" she asked.

"No. Don't even. I'm not wise. I've made so many mistakes in my life. In fact, I just spent the last few weeks trying to rectify a huge mistake I made years ago. I'm sure that much of my life is going to be spent trying to untangle the problems I've gotten myself into. I just hope I don't mess up Garnet's ministry, you know?"

"What do you mean?" Olive couldn't figure out what in the world she was talking about as she walked over and grabbed a glass from the cupboard, filling it up with water from the tap and taking a deep drink, grateful for the rest.

"I don't know. Maybe I'll say something that offends someone and they tell other people in the church and the church ends up splitting because of something I said carelessly. Or maybe there's someone who doesn't get along with me, and instead of giving in and being kind and loving and putting others first, I demand my own way. Maybe I don't even realize it, because you know I have a tendency to plow ahead with the things I want to do, and I don't always think about others. Maybe they'll think that I'm playing favorites. I've heard that a lot in churches. And I suppose it happens. But... You want to be kind to your friends and spend more time with people you really love, but it offends others you didn't even notice. It's just a balancing act, I think, and I'm not sure I'm up to it."

"You must be up to it. Since God gave you the job." That was all she could think to say as she rinsed the glass out and set it on the counter.

"I suppose you're right. Maybe He has more confidence in me than I do."

"Or maybe He knows that you know that you need to lean on Him. And that people are going to get angry, they're going to get upset, they're going to get offended, and that's not your fault."

"I suppose you're right."

"I know I am. When I think about how easily I've gotten offended over things, over stupid stuff that didn't really matter, but I felt like it did. You know? I could have been one of those people who split a church. Thankfully I never did, but as Christians, sometimes we just have no idea of how to be selfless and loving toward others and that the things that we fight about don't really matter. The color of the carpet for example."

"I know a church that split over the color of the carpet!" Mertie said, bringing her finger up and waving it around in the air. "I'm not even kidding."

"I believe it. It's ridiculous the things Christians fight over. Do you think the color of the carpet is going to matter five years from now? But yet, that church split will. There will be people who go to hell because the church split and people left angry. Children and grandchildren that might have been in church but won't be. And Christians allowed it to happen."

"That's so true. We don't think about the eternal consequences. We don't think about any of the consequences, not even to our own children. How does it look whenever we were insisting that we get our way because Mrs. So-and-so has overstepped her bounds and wasn't on the committee and shouldn't have any say in whether or not there are cushions on the pews."

They laughed together. But it really wasn't funny. How many more people would be Christians today if things like that, petty, ridiculous, non-biblical arguments, hadn't happened?

"But when we should stand up, when we should say no, when we should say that's not what the Bible says, we don't. So we let sin into the church, while we squabble over whether we have coffee or water in the foyer or whether our toilet paper is hung over or under, and meanwhile, sodomy has slipped into the church and we have pastors who are not biblically allowed to preach and murder is winked at and fornication and adultery are rampant, and people get offended if the pastor even whispers that it's sin, and yet...we allow it."

Mertie was so right, and all Olive could do was sit there and pray that she wasn't one of those people who was squabbling about stuff that didn't matter while major sin was overtaking the church and she wasn't doing anything about it. There were people who needed to be in church, but they'd left because they couldn't get along with each other.

"Sometimes ladies argue about how the church should be decorated for Christmas or spring, who should bring the flowers, and whether or not they brought the appropriate bouquet, or whether they bought a cheap one from the grocery store. Who cares?" Mertie shook her head.

They gave each other sad looks as a distracted Garnet came into the kitchen.

"I'm sorry about that. I think I'm going to need to go visit them. Do you think you can handle Norma Jean by yourself?"

"I know Miles is going to be disappointed, but I can definitely handle Norma Jean." Mertie rose and went over, putting her arms around him, while he hugged her close.

"I'm sorry. I almost asked him to go with me, but I don't think he's ready for that. And I'm not sure this is going to have a happy ending."

"My heart just breaks for those parents. What a difficult thing to go through."

"I think that they understand they probably should have been paying a little bit more attention to what their son was doing online, but he fell in with the wrong crowd and he's pretty determined that his parents are idiots and he's right and he's leaving. I... I don't know what to do. It's not the parents I need to talk to, and the son isn't listening."

There was a heaviness in the room that hadn't been there before. Olive supposed that this kind of stress really weighed on a person, when they felt the stress and heartbreak of everyone in their congregation, and some people who weren't even a part of it, as they tried to help them navigate the difficult things in life.

She hadn't realized how stressful it was to be a pastor, all she had thought was that they had to get a sermon up for Sunday morning and possibly one for Sunday evening. Maybe they taught the Sunday school lesson, but she hadn't realized that all of these other things took up their time.

"I'll see you later, but we're still getting married tomorrow, no matter what happens. Although, I do have a couple of people I should visit in the assisted living center after we go and Henry Johnson is in the hospital in Blueberry Beach. Maybe we can swing by and pray with him for a few minutes."

Mertie nodded. "That's all fine. I'll grab some groceries too, so we can plan on that stop as well."

They nodded, and they walked out the door together, Mertie chatting with Garnet, then he kissed her cheek. Olive buckled Livvy in the back seat while they said a few more words.

She was in with her seat belt on when Mertie finally said goodbye and opened the car door.

"I'm sorry."

"Not a problem. I... I didn't realize what you're getting into."

"Yeah, definitely being a Christian speaker and author is an easier lifestyle, although there are pressures with that as well. I still get emails almost daily from people who are asking me to give them advice, and all I can do is point to the Bible. They often don't want that. They want a magic bullet. An easy fix, and they don't realize that the problems that they're having are because of sin that has been going on for years oftentimes." She started the car and backed it out, turning it around and driving down the driveway ahead of Garnet.

Fourteen

Doyle parked his car in Miles's driveway and got out, trying to decide whether he should go to the house or to the barn.

He didn't expect Miles to be in the house at this time of day. Especially since he'd tried to call him several times and was unable to get an answer, so he decided to come and talk to him in person.

It wasn't an emergency, but he and Miles had done a few jobs together on Miles's farm, and Miles had done a few jobs on some of the properties that Doyle managed. He considered them friends. The fact that Miles wasn't answering his phone told Doyle that Miles was in the middle of a project and wasn't stopping and probably didn't have his phone on him.

Finally he decided that he might as well go in the house and ask, since if Miles wasn't in the barn he could be anywhere on the hundred or so acres that he owned, and it might save him some time if he could get directions from his wife.

He knew that Miles and Norma Jean didn't have the best relationship. Miles had mentioned something about a marriage of convenience, and Doyle took that to mean that they hadn't maybe known each other when they got married? Or maybe they weren't in love? He had his own opinions about what being in love meant and the mistakes people made when they got married because they thought that that was a good reason.

In his mind, in love just meant they were very close to being in lust, and it wasn't a great foundation on which to build a lifetime relationship. Friendship, shared interests, shared values even more than shared interests, and those types of things were the best foundation for marriage in his mind.

But he admitted that he could be wrong. Lately he'd been thinking that maybe it was just more important that both people have their eyes on Jesus and be following him. It was helpful for them to like each other and to be friends, but maybe it wasn't necessary. Maybe Jesus was all they needed.

He liked that idea and thought it was probably pretty accurate. He knocked on the door, and Norma Jean must have been in the kitchen because she answered almost immediately.

"Sorry to bother you, ma'am, but I was looking for your husband. He's not answering his phone."

"I hope it's not an emergency."

"No. I've just been working inside all morning, and when I couldn't reach him, I figured I'd come and see him."

She twisted her hands in front of her and swallowed. "I see. Well, I hate to admit that he doesn't really tell me what he's doing, but I know that he's been working on the fence behind the barn. He has phone service, but he usually takes his phone off and sets it somewhere so it doesn't get in his way. I think that's where you'll find him."

"Thanks, ma'am." He winked at the little girl that peeked out from behind a chair, looking at him with big eyes and a sweet little heart-shaped face.

Would that be how Livvy would look when she got a little older?

The baby had been so adorable. And he could easily see Olive all over her features. Of course, the dark, almost black eyes came from her dad. But he understood what Olive had said. That she had made a mistake. He didn't like it, it hurt him still to think about it, but he understood. He certainly made his share of mistakes, although hopefully not mistakes like that.

Of course, he knew it was easy for a person to look at someone else's mistakes and say, "that's a terrible mistake," judging them, when in reality, the mistakes that he made were just as bad. He had done that so many times in his life. Or looked at someone else and said to himself, "I would never do that," and then the next thing he knew, he was doing that like he'd never done that before.

It was almost like God had to teach someone a lesson when they thought something like that.

He shoved his hat back down on his head and stepped off the porch into the bright sunlight, taking a moment to realize that a car had pulled in while he had been talking to Norma Jean.

He thought he recognized it as Mertie's car, Olive's sister. But he wasn't expecting to see Olive pop out of the passenger seat. She had said that she was going to be helping her sisters fix up the house, not visiting the neighbors.

But sometimes plans changed, he supposed.

He walked down the walk, waved at Mertie, and stopped beside Olive. "I wasn't expecting to see you here."

He wasn't accusing her of anything, hopefully he was just making conversation, although he was curious as to how she ended up here.

"Yes, I know I said I was going to be helping my sisters fix up the mansion, but things changed for Mertie and Garnet, and I told Mertie I would come here with her."

"I see."

"What's going on with you?" she asked, and her tone was not demanding, like he owed her an explanation or anything of the sort. She seemed almost humble. Or maybe curious, like the care a friend might show.

He appreciated that. It felt good to have someone care.

"I had a project come up that I thought Miles might be interested in. He's helped me a few other times, and I thought of him immediately when it came across my desk this morning. He's not answering his phone, and it's a beautiful day out, so I decided that it might be beneficial for me to take a drive."

"Oh. It is a beautiful day. I have been enjoying my time out."

But she looked exhausted. He wanted to tell her that he thought she should go home and lie down, but he figured she probably wouldn't appreciate him saying that. He just didn't want her to overdo it and get worse instead of better. Sometimes it was hard for people to slow down, to realize that their body just needed time to rest and recover.

He was a good one to talk and really couldn't say anything. Plus, he didn't really have that right.

"All right then, I'll see you at supper?"

She nodded and smiled a little, which he returned. He didn't know about her, but he was thinking about their conversation where he had insisted that her meals were included in her employment package, and he wanted her to eat.

But then, when he would have turned away, something kept his gaze molded with hers. Something...elusive, that he couldn't name, but made him unable to turn away.

It was like the rest of the world faded away and it was just the two of them together.

Even when they were younger, he couldn't remember so completely losing track of everything else and just being focused on her. He wanted to put his hand out, touch her shoulder, pull her closer to him, maybe kiss her?

"Olive?" Her sister's voice interrupted them. "If you want to stay out here and talk to Doyle, that's fine, I can go in by myself."

He shook his head and stepped back, while Olive seemed to need a second or two to shake the cobwebs from her brain as well.

"Oh goodness. You got Livvy out, and I didn't even notice."

"You were talking. It was the least I could do. But if you want to keep talking, it's fine."

"No, no," she said, reaching out for the car seat.

Mertie seemed to be thinking along the same lines as Doyle was, and she pulled it away. "I can carry her."

Olive must have been just as tired as what he thought she was, since she didn't even argue with her sister.

Mertie's eyes met his as they walked away, with her lifting her brows in a silent question and him giving a slight nod of his head. He thought they were agreeing that neither one of them thought that Olive was in very good shape, and they would try to baby her as much as they could.

He wondered then if Mertie had really needed to come to do the Bible study, or if she was just trying to make sure that Olive took it easy.

Regardless, it didn't matter either way, he just knew that Olive needed more time to get better. And he was going to try to make sure that she got it, although he honestly couldn't say why it was so important to him.

Fifteen

Mertie dropped Olive off before Doyle had made it home. Olive knew that because his truck was still sitting there at Norma Jean and Miles's house when they left. And Mertie took her right home.

"Are you nervous about your wedding tomorrow?" she asked, knowing that she would be. A lifetime was a long time to pledge to someone else. How did she know it was the right person? How did she know that she was going to be able to keep the vows that she was going to make before God? How did she know that the person she was going to marry wasn't going to change and morph into someone else over the years?

"No. I have absolute confidence that this is what God wants for me. I would be foolish to not."

"How do you have that confidence?" she asked, knowing she should have gotten out of the car and gone into the house. If she wanted to talk to her sister, she should have done it earlier, but now she was holding her up.

"I suppose with years of Bible study, prayer, and definitely getting Scripture into your mind every way you can, but...sometimes God just works things out in such a way that you know."

"I wish you could explain that."

"You might read Scripture that tells you, you might have a friend that you trust who says something that seems like an answer. You might get advice from other people who are saying the same thing. Or maybe the events line up in your life, one thing falls into place after another, and you're just sure of it. But I think maybe when you get saved, the Holy Spirit comes and dwells in you. It says so in Acts. And when you sin, if you're paying attention, the Holy Spirit will make you feel guilty for that sin. You feel bad when you grieve the Holy Spirit. Because obviously, the Holy Spirit can't stand sin. So if you're doing something right, you have a feeling of peace, total absence of concern and fear. It will just feel exactly right, and you'll know that God is in it. I suppose, it's just the way sometimes you wake up in the morning and you don't even have to open your eyes and you know it's light out, you know? The sunshine is there, and you can see it without opening your eyes."

"I see. I guess I've never been that sure about anything."

"Maybe you've never asked God to show you and lead you."

"I suppose I haven't. I've been more interested in doing things my own way." Although she did definitely feel like coming back to the United States and to Raspberry Ridge was the exact right decision. Maybe that was the confidence that a person had when God was in control.

"I just wish I would have spent more of my life doing what God wanted than what I wanted."

"You can't look at the past and regret it. You can look at the past and learn from it, but spend as little time as possible in the past. You can't change it. God still has work for you to do because you're still here, so don't be discouraged, don't think that there's nothing left for you, just open your eyes, look around you at the work in front of you, and then put your hand to the plow, whatever it is, and just do it with all your heart."

"I don't know if I've ever said this to you, but I'm so thankful that you're my sister. I think there are a lot of people who wish that they had access to you the way I do. I'm blessed." And she hadn't taken the time to be thankful for it nearly as much as what she should have.

"I think that's me. You're a great sister, and not everyone has someone who is so well-traveled in their family."

"I don't think it compares, but okay," she said, yanking the handle and pushing out the door. "Thanks a lot for taking me today, I appreciate it," she said, slamming the door shut and then opening the back door so she could get her baby.

"I appreciate you rolling with the change of plans, and I'm sorry I forgot to call."

"You're getting married tomorrow. You have a lot of things going on. I'm certainly not upset that you forgot one little thing like a phone call to me."

"Lesser things have split a church," Mertie said, and they grinned at the reference to their earlier conversation.

Mertie waved, Olive shut the door, and she drove off.

What God had for her to do. Right where she was.

She looked around at the slightly crumbling house and figured that maybe when she had a little bit more time and energy, she would talk to Doyle about fixing it up. She didn't have a whole lot of experience in that type of thing, but she'd done her share of impromptu electrical and plumbing bandages at the various places she'd stayed around the world. Surely, with online videos at her fingertips, she could fix this old house.

As she walked up the walk, she saw that Cassie sat on the porch.

Look around you, see what God has right in front of you.

She was exhausted, her feet hurt, and her back between her shoulder blades ached, but Cassie was who God had right in front of her, and instead of being a light to Cassie, she'd almost acted like they were enemies.

"Is it okay if I sit down?" she asked, nodding at the chair that sat slightly at an angle to Cassie's.

"Sure. I thought you and Doyle were out together."

"Well, actually we kind of were, although it was an accident."

"Really?" Cassie said, lifting her brows, her dark eyes holding suspicion.

"Yeah, I expected to be going to my sisters' house to help get it ready to sell. When I got there, Mertie was on her way to Miles and Norma Jean's house to do Bible study. When we got there, Doyle was already there, just coming down the walk. I assume he was...maybe asking where

Miles was? Anyway, he was there the whole time I was, but I didn't see him again."

"What's between you two?" Cassie asked, and her question seemed to hold a little bit of accusation. It ruffled Olive's feathers, but she tried to rein her irritation in. She was going to be kind. She could hardly show love if she was irritated.

"We were together for a little bit years ago. We both grew up here in Raspberry Ridge."

"Such a cute little town," Cassie said, and it almost could have been an insult, but Olive kind of thought she might have meant it. "Sorry. Didn't mean to interrupt you. Go on. You grew up here. So you've known each other forever."

"Yeah, pretty much. We went to the same church forever, and we played together, since we were the only two kids our age in town. I had a sister who was older and a younger sister, and he had an older sister too."

"He does?"

"I think I heard she passed away." She hadn't thought about her in a long time and certainly not since she'd come home. There were too many other things on her mind, and now she felt bad. She should have talked to Doyle about it immediately.

"That's too bad. I didn't know."

"If you were his housekeeper in Chicago, I think it was just a few years ago."

"If it was, he never said. He didn't usually talk to me too much."

"I see."

"Anyway, you guys were together since you were little?"

"No. We were friends, and I guess after our senior year of high school, we felt like we were more. I came up for the summer, and we were kind of a couple for a few months, but... I didn't want to stay in town. I had big dreams of traveling the world, and I don't really know what his plans were. Stay in Raspberry Ridge and get a job and be happy."

"Well, he's done far more than that. You know he's rich, right?"

This news did shock Olive, although she tried to hide just how much. She had never been interested in Doyle for his money. When they'd been together, he didn't have any.

"I didn't really know what he was doing. I assumed he could afford to pay me what he said he was going to, and he didn't seem to think hard to put you on the payroll either. But beyond that, I guess I hadn't thought about it."

"Well, he was into managing some properties. He was good at it, and he ended up with his own business. I know that much at least. He seems to be doing pretty well for himself anyway. His place in Chicago was really, really nice. This is dumpy compared to that."

Olive almost felt like she and Cassie were having a regular conversation. The kind of conversation two friends might have. Two people who weren't antagonistic toward each other and at each other's throats constantly. She didn't want to examine it too much or cause Cassie to forget who she was talking to and go back to her not-very-nice treatment.

"Is this where he lived growing up?" Cassie asked while Olive was still trying to figure out what to say about the dumpy comment.

"No. They had a house along Main Street. But I think his dad was from Canada, and his parents moved back there not long after we graduated."

"I can't believe he didn't move back with them."

"I don't think they were very close. He told me once he thought he was adopted, but I never really talked to him about that."

"I see."

"Why are you here?" She figured she might as well be as blunt as what Cassie had been being. And just hope she didn't offend her.

"You probably wouldn't understand."

"Try me."

Livvy fussed a little, and she prayed silently that Livvy would stay asleep long enough for her to have a conversation with Cassie. She liked this feeling that maybe they could be friends. Which surprised her since she wouldn't have said that at all after their first interactions together, when Cassie seemed to be trying to push her aside.

"You have your sisters, a nice little relationship with them, and this cute town where everyone knows your name and loves you. The city isn't like that."

"You have family there. Doyle said so anyway."

"It's not the same. We're not close, and my friends are a lot more cutthroat...kind of the way I was when I first came. But you... You didn't let me push you out, but you were kind to me when I wasn't kind to you. It's like you didn't allow me trying to take your job to bother you. And I can only figure out that that was because you had the support system of your sisters in this town."

"Well, it's more like I have the Lord. Whatever He works out, I just know He's going to take care of me."

"That's ridiculous. I wouldn't have pegged you as someone who believed in fairy tales. I mean, it's one thing to go to church. That's like a community or whatever, but it's another thing to actually believe that."

"You don't have to if you don't want to, but I do." She looked at her shoulder. Not sure what else to say. It wasn't exactly the best time to get into a whole explanation of the Bible and what she believed.

"Christians are supposed to love everyone. I guess that's what you were trying to do when you were nice to me."

"I think it goes a little bit further than that, you know, the golden rule and all of that."

"Do unto others as you would have them do unto you?" Cassie said with a laugh in her voice. "That never works."

"I don't know that it's necessarily something that you're trying to get to work. It's just a rule to live by. If everyone lived by it, the world would be a better place."

"It sure would, but if you're not going to live by it, I'm not going to waste my time living by it either."

"I guess that's where we differ. I believe in a God who loves me and who takes care of me but also wants me to do good things, not so I can get to heaven, that's not the way—"

"What is the way?"

Olive hesitated. She hated it when people asked her this question, or she got into this situation. She never knew what to say. And she was afraid that what she would say would sound stupid and would drive them away from the Lord instead of leading them to Him.

But God could direct her words and control how they hit Cassie's heart. She decided that the best thing to do was to just answer the question honestly.

"Jesus said, 'I am the way, the truth, and the life: no man cometh unto the father, but by me.' So Jesus is the way."

"What does that mean? Like, where is Jesus? How do you get to heaven when he's dead, right?"

"No, actually he's not. They did kill him, but He came back to life, and I know," she put her hand up, "that sounds crazy, but there are witnesses. In history, historical witnesses who saw Him be crucified and then saw Him rise from the dead. There are other witnesses who saw the empty tomb. And just in case you think they are lying because they don't want to be proved wrong, every single one of His eleven disciples saw Him after He was crucified and died a martyr's death saying that He came back to life and teaching other people to believe in Him."

Cassie's brows raised. "They must have really believed it if they were willing to die for it."

"Not too many people are willing to die for what they believe. So yeah. I think they were pretty sure they were right, and since they were eyewitnesses, they most likely were."

"So you didn't answer my question about how to go through Jesus."

"I guess that's it. The reason that he died is because there had to be a perfect shed blood sacrifice for our sins. And he was the only one who could do it."

"A shed blood sacrifice? That's stupid."

"I didn't make the rules. I guess if I had, it wouldn't have been that. But God created the world, made the universe, created you and me, and if He said there needs to be a shed blood sacrifice, then I'm just gonna believe Him."

"So Jesus died, what does that have to do with me?"

"That's really it. You just have to believe that you're a sinner, repent from your sins, which is probably something that we don't do a whole lot today, but repentance is necessary before salvation. You can't just say, 'Yeah, I'm a sinner, and I'm gonna keep sinning, but I'm gonna believe in Jesus, and he can save me.' We have to turn from our sins. Admit that they're wrong and that we're going to try not to sin anymore."

"So that's why Christians are always goody two-shoes."

"I guess if you look at it that way. But I look at it more like the fact that my sin caused Jesus to have to go to the cross. And when Jesus was on the cross, he was paying the payment for the sin of the world. I don't want to add to that sin. I don't want to put more on his shoulders. He already did more for me than I could ever repay him for. The very least I could do is to try to live a life that pleases him and hopefully leads others to him, just because I'm different."

"Well, I guess that's why I'm sitting here talking to you. Anyone else I know would have been angry and mean to me because of the way I treated them and the way I tried to take your job. But instead of being unkind, you came here and sat down and started chatting with me like we're friends. I don't have any friends here in Raspberry Ridge, and I thought I would be okay because... I really like Doyle. But it wasn't the way I thought it was going to be. And I'm lonely."

Olive blinked. She wasn't expecting any of this. Not this conversation, not the opportunity to present the gospel to Cassie, and not the idea that Cassie was going to admit that she was lonely.

"You have a friend here." She took a breath. "In me. I don't say that lightly. Being a friend is more than just waving a hand and popping in and out of someone's life. Being a friend is...being there when somebody needs you and doing whatever they need you to do. All they have to do is ask."

"I've never really had a friend like that. My friends are there when they want something, and they disappear if I can't do anything for them."

"I can say that I try not to be that kind of friend. I probably am not very successful. In fact, you can probably find a hundred people who will tell you that I'm a failure more than I'm a success, but... I'm here for you, and if I can do it for you, I will."

"Please leave," Cassie said, lifting her brows in challenge.

Olive blinked. Had that been a trap all along? Had she been stringing her along just to ditch her like that? "Really? That's what you need me to do as your friend?"

"Yeah. If you will try to do whatever you can for me, if you're truly my friend, leave. You're distracting Doyle from focusing on me. Without you, he would be interested in me like he was before."

Those words struck down into Olive's soul. Doyle had been interested in Cassie? "I didn't know that you two were a thing."

"We were never together, but we were almost together. That was before he decided to move here."

"Did he ask you if you wanted to, and you said no?"

"No. I think he was running from me because he was scared of commitment. He doesn't have to be afraid."

"I see. So... You want me to leave, quit my job, and have no place to stay and no money coming in just because we're friends?" Olive was finding it a little bit hard to breathe. And she was finding it difficult to believe that she was actually thinking about doing this, just to show Cassie that she meant what she said.

"Yeah. You just said that's what friends do, sacrifice whatever and whenever their friends need them. I need you to leave. How good of a friend are you?"

She didn't think that Cassie was being mean. And she didn't think that Cassie was trying to hurt her, she was just trying to get her way and trying to manipulate her, using her own words against her in order to do that.

"All right. Will you watch my baby while I go in and pack my things?"

Cassie's mouth dropped open, and her eyes opened wide. "You're serious?"

"If I'm in the way of you getting what you want. You want Doyle, and you want me out. If we're friends, and we just said we were, then... I have to leave."

She couldn't believe she was saying that. She didn't want to go, but she knew she had a place where she could stay. Her sisters wouldn't mind at all if she stayed in their parents' house until they sold it. She'd have to leave every time they showed it, but plenty of people lived in a house that was for sale and went somewhere if a realtor had a potential buyer who wanted to tour the house.

"You would actually leave?" Cassie asked again, sounding like she couldn't believe it.

"Sure. Will you watch the baby?" She nodded at the car seat where Livvy slept. Someday, Livvy was going to start being awake more than she was asleep, and she would be a lot harder to take care of, but for now, Olive just appreciated the fact that she wasn't a difficult baby at all.

"Yes. I'll watch her."

She looked like she didn't believe Olive was actually going to go in and pack her things, but Olive had every intention in the world of doing exactly what she had said she was going to do.

Maybe this was what Mertie meant when she said you would have a complete peace when it was the Lord's will, because that's what she had. Knowledge that what she was doing was exactly the right thing.

It didn't take long to gather up the few things she had. It actually took longer to grab the baby's things, and she felt a little guilty as she took the formula that Doyle had purchased at the beginning of the week. Hopefully the hours that she had worked would cover the payment for that. But she wasn't sure.

"I've never quit a job without giving a notice before. Will you please cover my shift for breakfast and lunch until Doyle can find someone else?"

"Yeah." Cassie stood as she came out. "I'll cover it. I can't believe you're leaving."

"You asked me to," she said as she set the stuff down on the porch and thought about how far it was from where she was to her parents' house on the hill. Hoping she had the energy to make it the whole way. Her stomach growled as well, but maybe there was food at the mansion. She prayed there was.

If not, Cassie was right, she could call her sisters. They would help her. She didn't want to. She wanted to be able to stand on her own two feet, but she did have the luxury of having sisters who cared about her and wouldn't allow her to starve to death or sleep on the streets.

"See you around. Maybe in church on Sunday," she said as she picked up the baby in one hand, her bag in the other, and prayed that she could make it to the mansion.

"Yeah. I'll be there," Cassie said, her voice subdued as she watched her walk off, although Olive had hoped that she would call her back, and she didn't.

Grateful that she did not pass Doyle on his way home before she made it out of the driveway and down the street of Raspberry Ridge, she crossed the street and started to walk up her drive.

Had she done the right thing? She really wished that she would have been able to explain to Doyle what was going on, because she wasn't sure that Cassie would tell him the truth. In fact, she highly suspected that Cassie would either say nothing or make up a lie, because how could Cassie say that she had asked Olive to leave and Olive had?

Regardless, she was strangely unconcerned. Maybe that was because of her faith in the Lord, or maybe that was just because she was so tired.

Sixteen

D oyle pulled into the drive, exhausted, covered in sweat and dirt, and looking forward to spending a little bit of time with Olive. He didn't even mind the idea of spending some time with the little one. In fact, he had to admit he was looking forward to that too.

They finished the fence, and Miles had agreed to help him out with the job he needed. They'd even talked about marriage a little, although Doyle didn't feel like he had any good advice to give Miles. Still, he listened as Miles talked about what the pastor had told him the last time he was out. It all sounded like good advice to Doyle. In fact, it was advice he might be able to use someday. Maybe someday that wasn't too far away, although Olive still hadn't shown any sign of being the slightest bit interested in him.

He walked into the house. It smelled amazing, and he had to hand it to Cassie. She was an excellent cook. She was serving the Parmesan-crusted carrots again; he could see their orange color as he stepped into the kitchen to greet her and wash his hands.

"This smells good." He stuck his hands under the water after squirting some soap on them and rubbing them together.

"Thanks. If you don't mind, I'm going to eat with you tonight."

"Sure. As soon as I finish washing up here, I'll go get Olive. She's probably tired, maybe taking a nap."

"She's gone."

He paused, thinking that he must have misheard Cassie. "I thought you said she was gone."

"I did. She left."

"She left. For good?" he asked, trying to reconcile what Cassie was telling him to the Olive he had just spoken with earlier that day. She hadn't mentioned anything about leaving. It hadn't looked like she had any intentions of going anywhere, and... They'd had that moment.

Maybe that had scared her. It certainly had rocked his world. There was still something there after all these years, and he wanted to figure out what it was. Maybe she... She'd always been kind of commitment shy, afraid to stay in one place for long. She said she changed but... Maybe she hadn't after all.

"Yep. For good."

"You know why?" He knew he probably shouldn't ask Cassie. She had not exactly been friends with Olive.

"Because I asked her to."

"What?" He couldn't help it; his voice raised a little.

"I asked her to." Cassie lifted her shoulder. "It was too much to have the two of us here. You were having trouble paying attention to both of us, and I decided that it would be best if one of us left. I asked for it to be her, and she agreed."

That sounded a little fishy, but he couldn't quite put his finger on what was wrong.

"So you asked her to leave, because I couldn't give both of you enough attention?"

"You couldn't give me enough attention, because you were so focused on her." Cassie folded her arms across her midsection and turned to look at him, defiantly almost, daring him to contradict her.

"I hired you to be my housekeeper. Not my relationship police."

"Well, maybe I want to be more."

He drew back, almost as though she had tried to smack him.

"Maybe I don't." He said the words slowly, carefully, realizing that he was traversing some type of land mine that he hadn't been expecting.

"Oh, come on, you know you do. We were really getting close in Chicago, before you left."

"I left because I wanted to move here, and you made me uncomfortable."

"I knew it." She looked triumphant. "I knew that I had scared you."

"You tried to kiss me."

"And you were scared. You're afraid. But there's no need. You don't need to be afraid of me. We can have something really good together."

"But I don't want that." He wasn't sure how to say it so that she would understand. Yes, she was right, she had scared him, but not in a "I think I really like her, but I don't want to have a commitment" kind of way, the way she seemed to think. It was more of a "this girl is taking liberties that I don't want her to have and trying to be closer to me than I'm comfortable with, not because I like her, but because I don't like her that" way.

How could he tell her that?

"Really? You're a man. You don't know what you want. That's why I'm here to tell you. You want me, we're good together. We can be even better. You just have to let your guard down and let me in." She smiled reassuringly, and he supposed that was supposed to make him do something, but he wasn't sure what it was.

"I don't like you that way. I never will. I am uncomfortable with this whole situation, not because I like you and you're making me uncomfortable, but because I don't. I feel like our relationship is purely professional, and you've crossed some lines."

"Didn't you hear me? You're a man. You don't know what you want."

"Oh no. I promise you, I know what I want, and it's not you." He didn't want to be mean, he didn't want to shove her away with no ceremony, but this was getting a little bit ridiculous.

"Did Olive say where she was going?" He didn't know how to handle what Cassie was throwing at him, and getting out of the house seemed like the best thing.

"No, not really. But she has sisters, and this whole town loves her. She's probably around somewhere, with one of her friends or with her sisters. Maybe at her parents' house?" Cassie held a spoon in her hand

and leaned against the counter, like she hadn't thrown the woman he...
was fond of...out of his house.

"I guess that's a good place to start looking." He finished drying off
his hands and hung the towel up before turning around and facing her.
"I think it might be best if you were gone when I get back."

"Doyle. You don't mean that."

He put a hand up. "I know. I'm a man. I don't know what I want,
except I do. I want you to be gone when I get back. If you need money
or a ride, I can help you out, but you can't stay here."

He wasn't sure if that was the right thing to do or not. She could
stay there. It wasn't going to bother him, but she couldn't keep making
passes at him and kicking people out that he'd invited to stay.

"Where am I going to go?" she asked softly, and doggone it, he hated
it when women cried, and her eyes were filling with tears.

"Listen, I don't care if you stay. I don't care if you continue to be my
housekeeper, but that's all it is. You being a housekeeper. I don't want
these uncomfortable confrontations where you have this weird idea that
there is more between us. Because there is not. I'm fine if you stay, fine if
you go, but I'm not fine if you ask someone to leave after I've asked
them to stay, and I'm not okay if you keep confronting me about
whatever thing you think is between us. Because it's only on your side, I
promise you."

He thought he was as clear as he could be, and it seemed like she
understood, because she nodded slowly.

"I'm gonna stay."

He nodded, then looked around. "I'm going to go find Olive."

"Aren't you going to eat first?"

"No. If you want to, go ahead. I'll skip supper, and we'll talk about
breakfast in the morning, depending on where Olive is."

He found that he was getting angry. It was a delayed reaction
apparently. Because Olive shouldn't have left, and Cassie shouldn't have
asked her to. He wasn't sure which woman he was more angry at.

Olive probably. Just because his emotions toward her were sharper,
stronger, and more tender. She'd left him once before, and surely she
knew how he would feel about her leaving again, even though they
weren't supposed to be in a relationship. Plus, she could have told

him. She could have talked to him about it. She didn't have to just walk out.

Yeah, definitely Olive was the one he was the most angry at.

He probably should take a shower, but he felt an urgency to find her immediately. The first place he was going to look was the mansion; if she wasn't there, he was going to find one of her sisters and talk to them.

He was out the door and halfway to his truck when he realized that he could just call her.

Man, for a child of the twenty-first century, he was a little bit dense. He couldn't believe he hadn't thought of his phone up until that point.

Pulling up her contact, he pressed the call button, realizing as he did so that maybe she wouldn't pick up.

But it had only rung three times before she answered.

"Hello?"

"Olive. You left me. Again."

"I'm sorry. I have a big long text that I had written out, but I didn't send it because it sounded dumb."

"A big long text? Telling me why you left?"

"I didn't want to talk about why," she said softly.

"Because Cassie asked you to?"

"She told you that?" It was Olive's turn to sound shocked.

"She did. What? Didn't you think she'd admit it?" He got in his truck, waiting until his phone connected to the truck speakers before he put it in reverse and backed out of the drive.

"No. I thought she'd make something up."

"We can talk about it later. I'm on my way to wherever you are. Where is that?" he asked, realizing that he really didn't know, he was just taking off and going somewhere, probably because there was a part of him that just couldn't stand not doing anything.

"I'm at the mansion. By myself, but I'm fine. You don't have to come."

"I'm on my way. I'll be there in a couple minutes."

He almost hung up, because he didn't want her to tell him not to come, but he didn't want to lose that connection.

"Did she really just ask you to leave?"

"It's a little bit more involved than that. I had just told her that I would be her friend, and that was after I had given her the gospel. I... I didn't feel like I could refuse her request because it felt like she was testing me. Was I really going to be a friend? Was I really going to be there for her like I had just said I would be?"

"She has friends and family in Chicago."

"She said it wasn't like here. And she's right, what I have with my sisters... We're not as close as we could be, but I know I could depend on them to do anything for me. I could call them up right now, ask them to do anything, and they would."

He could not believe it. She was right; Cassie's family in Chicago was spread out and not exactly the nicest people he knew, but still, how Olive had figured that out and had known that she needed to show true friendship, keeping her word, was beyond him.

"It still makes me angry that you left. You know, she was probably just working you."

"But I needed to do what I said I was going to do. Whether she was working me or not. If I'm a friend, it can't matter what other people do to me, I have to just continue to be a friend. Right?"

Wow. She was supposed to be the one who had walked away from the Lord and done her own thing, and he was supposed to be the one who was the rock, but she had just taught him a lesson. His actions shouldn't change based on what other people did to him, and yet... So often they did.

"You're right. And I definitely can learn from you how to handle people, or how to handle myself, more like it."

Seventeen

Doyle turned into her driveway, moving up the lane. Olive was still on the phone, and he was trying to figure out how to get her to come back.

"Is it okay if I come in and visit for a little bit?" he asked, humbly, knowing that he didn't have any right to demand that she return, and he hadn't even been as good a friend to her as what she'd been to Cassie.

"Of course. I'm on the back porch, if you just want to come on through. I have Livvy on my lap, and she is enjoying the lake view, I believe."

"She's going to fall in love with the lake before she's old enough to talk," he said, knowing that because he'd grown up beside the lake, it would always have a piece of his heart.

"Maybe. It's beautiful, and it definitely reminds us of God's majesty."

"That's probably the best thing about it," he said as he shut his pickup off and waited for his phone to disconnect from the truck before he got out. "Is the door unlocked?"

"It is. And it's just me here. I talked to Mertie earlier, and Garnet had been called out for someone who is having emergency surgery. He's at the hospital now praying with the family, and she is staying with his parents."

"Aren't they supposed to get married tomorrow?"

"They are, and I'm pretty sure they're still going to, but it might be between trips to the hospital. Garnet has been pretty busy. I hope things slow down for them."

"Me too." It would be terrible to start out married life like that, just thrust into the thick of things. But Garnet seemed to be handling it well, and Mertie had experience in ministry, even if it wasn't in exactly a small-town church ministry.

He walked in, noting the clean kitchen and the fresh smell of paint. The house looked like they had been getting it ready for sale, and he couldn't help but note the differences between this house and the one he was renting.

His steps slowed as an idea came to him.

Could he do that?

He put a hand on the counter and looked around. This was more house than he would ever need, but he could more than afford it, whatever they were going to ask for it. He wouldn't even have to negotiate, and then...what? He would have Olive where he wanted her?

That wasn't exactly the way he wanted to think about it. It was more like he would have a home for her whenever she wanted it. But he would probably see about moving out of the house he was living in now, or even buying it, as had been his plan, and renting it out, and moving here. There wasn't a whole lot of things to move, and... He would have to talk to Olive about it. But more than that, he wanted to know if there was a chance for Olive and him.

Not because he was thinking about Cassie, and he probably needed to make that clear to her. Especially if Cassie had told her to leave because Cassie wanted him.

He pushed the door open and smiled at the sight of mother and daughter sitting on the porch, their faces lifted to the breeze, watching the sunset. The sun had already slipped below the horizon, but the sky was ablaze with colors stretching up as far as they could see.

"That's beautiful."

"It's one of the best things about this house. The lake reflects the sunset, and you have such a beautiful view of the sky, morning and night."

"With the reflection on the lake, it's almost like you get to see it twice." He paused to take in the horizon. "Definitely a beautiful view of the lake. I didn't realize you could see that well from this far out. Doesn't seem like that steep of a hill."

"Until you're walking with a car seat."

He looked at her, truly looked at her, for the first time. She looked a lot more ragged than she had even when he'd seen her a few hours ago at Miles and Norma Jean's place.

"You look exhausted."

"Before you called, I was thinking seriously about putting Livvy to bed and going there myself."

"Can I hold her for a little bit?" he asked, standing beside her and looking down, thinking at least he would take that burden away from her but realizing that he actually did want to hold the baby. Maybe he was feeling paternal instincts, or maybe it was just because of Olive, but he found himself realizing that if Olive were to move out of his life, he'd lose Livvy as well, and the thought made him sad.

"You can. But don't feel like you have to."

"I don't. I want to." The words were true, and he reached down as she held the baby out.

She gave him a big smile as she settled in his arms, almost like she recognized him.

"I think you and she developed a bond while I was sleeping the other day."

"She's a good baby. She only fussed when her diaper was dirty."

"I've been blessed. It could have been a lot worse, but she made everything so easy for me."

"You deserve something that's a little bit easy. After everything you went through."

"We have to face the consequences of our sin," she said seriously, and he didn't look away from the baby, even though he wanted to, to read what was on her face. He could hear the regret in her voice. That was enough for him. It made him feel bad, but she wasn't the only person with regrets.

"I told Cassie that I wanted her to leave, and she gave me a sob story about how she didn't have anyone in Chicago. Maybe that's what she gave you too?"

"Yeah. I felt bad for her."

"Well, I must have too, because I told her she could stay, but I didn't want any more...days like today. She...told me that with you gone, she and I could have a relationship, and I told her that I didn't want one. Not like that. That she was an employee, and I was her employer, and if she could remember that, she could stay. But I'll make her go if having her there will make you uncomfortable."

"It won't. Because I'm not there."

"I want you to come back," he said, and he heard the pleading in his voice but could not modulate it.

"I told her I would go." Olive sighed, like she didn't want to have this conversation. Or maybe she was too tired for it. "I'm not trying to say that to be smart or mean or difficult. I promise. I just had a whole conversation with her about Jesus and salvation and being Christian, and I told her I was her friend, and then she asked me to do something. Right after I had told her that any time she wanted me to do something, all she had to do was ask. How could I say no?"

"You did what she asked, and I told her that what she asked was unacceptable, and I'm asking you to come back."

She looked down. "I think that if I do, the opportunity for her to get saved will disappear."

"So you would stay away, just because you think that she might get saved?"

"If she sees that I really meant what I said, and I live what I believe, it might make her realize that it's a real thing."

"Or maybe she decided she doesn't want to be a Christian because you have to give up everything you want, or at least that's the way it looks."

"Isn't that the way it is?"

"It doesn't show that God changes what we want."

"That's not true. I wanted to leave. I wanted to do whatever was needed to in order for her to see that I meant it."

"How are you going to support yourself?" he asked as he shifted

Livvy just a bit. Her eyes seemed to be drooping, and he thought she might fall asleep. He rocked her gently in his arms.

"I don't know. I mean, I know that my sisters aren't going to let me starve, but the whole reason I was working there was because I didn't want to be dependent on them. I wanted to support myself."

"What if I bought this house?"

"This house?" she asked, like he hadn't been clear.

"Your house. Your parents' house. Isn't that what you guys are doing? Getting it ready to sell?"

"Yeah, but it's not for sale."

"And it doesn't need to be. You guys can get together with your appraiser or realtor or whatever, figure out how much you're going to ask for it, and I'll pay it. I'll stop renting the house that I'm in—"

"You're renting?"

"Yeah. I wasn't quite sure whether I was going to be coming to stay or not. And my year lease will be up in two months. That should be enough time for us to make the real estate sale go through here and perfect timing for me to move."

Her eyes closed, and he couldn't tell whether it was because she was tired or because she was praying.

"I can't stop you from buying it if that's what you want."

"Will you work for me if you work here? You left like Cassie asked you to, did everything she asked, and now you're off the hook."

"I didn't feel like I was on the hook though. That's just it."

"How about you think about it? It looks like you're tired right now, and I'm pushing you."

"Thank you. I am exhausted. I was just trying to get up the energy to put Livvy to bed."

"Has she had her bottle?"

"She has everything she needs, I changed her, put her sleeper on her, gave her her nightly bottle. All you have to do is put her down in her crib and walk away."

"She has a crib?"

"It's actually like a pack 'n play, and it's in the first room to the left at the top of the stairs." She sighed as she said it, like just talking was taxing her more than she had energy for.

He gave her a worried glance, then said, "I'll be right back."

He felt like he'd been pushing her, begging her to be with him, and she refused, but he tried not to take it personally. He understood what she was saying. Cassie's salvation was more important than Olive's comfort. And he wondered how many other Christians in the world were willing to give up so much in order to show someone else the way to salvation. Show them what a true Christian was. Show them what sacrifice and kindness and honor and keeping a person's word was. The loyalty of a friend. The loyalty that Jesus showed his disciples. Not the other way around.

He couldn't remember ever being that loyal and kind to a friend.

Unless a person counted Olive. Because, after the way she treated him when she left, he supposed he should have been mad at her, but he'd hired her. Still, he hadn't been as kind to her as she'd been to someone she barely knew and who hadn't been kind to her at all, at least not that Doyle had seen.

He cradled Livvy in his arms as he carried her up the stairs, her eyes drooping, her little fists tucked up underneath her chin.

Whatever had been in her young life that had taught her that crying was pointless made him feel terrible, but it definitely made him smile to see how content she seemed.

She barely stirred when he laid her down in the crib and grabbed the blanket that was in there, pulling it up and tucking it around her.

Her eyes blinked up at him, and she smiled just a little before she turned her head toward the wall and her eyes drifted shut again.

He kissed his fingers and tapped them gently on her forehead. She barely stirred.

"Good night, sweetheart," he said softly as he moved quietly to the door, closing it behind him.

What a precious baby, a baby with no dad, a baby here in his town, with the woman he admired, and he found he wanted to do everything in his power to make both of their lives easier.

Problem was, he had to convince her that she should let him in.

But then he remembered Cassie, trying to push and how he felt when he didn't want her. Was that what he was doing?

He came down and found Olive sitting in the same spot, only her eyes were closed and her head tilted to the side.

He had been trying to figure out which room was hers while he was upstairs, but he hadn't thought for a second that he might be carrying her to bed as well.

"I think someone else needs to go to bed," he said softly, and her eyes blinked open and she smiled sleepily. The sunset was fading, and it was getting dark, but it was light enough for him to see that there was complete trust in her eyes.

"Did she go okay?"

"She went perfectly." He paused. "I'm going to carry you up too."

"I can walk," she protested, but it was a weak protest.

"I didn't say you couldn't. I just announced what I was going to do."

She didn't protest again as he put his arms under her legs and another arm behind her back and lifted her carefully.

He just held her there for a moment, cradling her against him, surprised at how light she was.

He couldn't talk to her the way he wanted to, couldn't work things out, not right now, but he did need to ask one question.

"Am I pushing too hard to be with you?"

Her eyes popped open, and her brows drew down.

"What?"

"I just was thinking about Cassie and how she insisted that she wanted to be with me, and she made me uncomfortable because I didn't want to be with her like that. I want to be with you, but I wondered if I was pushing you the way Cassie was pushing me."

There was a ghost of a smile that came over her face as her eyes lowered.

She shook her head and whispered, "No."

That one word thrilled his soul and eased all the doubts that had been climbing up the back of his throat. All the thoughts that maybe he was trying too much, doing something that she didn't want to do, when she'd rather just be left alone.

Maybe there was hope after all.

Everything else would have to wait until another day, everything except for this. "Will you go with me to the wedding tomorrow?"

"I have to go early."

"I'll take you whatever time. Just text me, okay?"

"Okay."

"Actually, I just might stay downstairs, you...seem tired."

"You don't have to. You probably didn't bring anything, and...it wouldn't look very good."

"I guess I don't really care how it looks, if I feel like you need it." He understood the verse that said to avoid all appearance of evil, but if someone needed him, he wasn't going to stand on ceremony. Especially if that someone was Olive.

"Thank you," she said softly as he grabbed the door, pulling it open and slipping inside then allowing it to close behind him. Careful not to bump her head.

In the time that they'd spent together back when they were together, he'd never carried her anywhere, and he found that he loved the closeness, the feeling of protecting her and taking care of her, and just having her next to him.

Her hand rested on his chest, and her face pressed against him as well.

He really didn't want to set her down.

"Which bedroom is yours?" he asked as he mounted the steps a second time.

"Across the hall from Livvy," she said, and he had to lean low in order to hear her whispered words.

He opened the door to her room, carried her in, and removed her shoes before putting a blanket over top of her.

He leaned down and pressed his lips to her forehead. Holding them there for just a moment longer than strictly necessary, breathing in her scent, and wishing that he didn't have to go.

"Night," he said softly.

"Night," she repeated quietly.

Against everything that he wanted to do, he straightened, turning toward the door and walking. Deciding that he would indeed sleep on the couch and be up early in the morning, maybe checking on Livvy before he left. But Olive had no car, and he just felt better being here to make sure she was okay.

Eighteen

Olive stretched. Memories from last night vaguely came back to her, although she felt so tired. Like she just couldn't get enough sleep, but she wasn't sleepy. She was pretty sure she had gotten up with Livvy once, and then she vaguely thought that perhaps Doyle had gotten up with her once too. She seemed to remember him standing in the doorway in the dark, asking about how much formula to feed.

She couldn't even remember what answer she had given.

Hopefully the right one. Hopefully she answered him. Or was it just a dream?

Her limbs felt like they weighed a million pounds, though she could tell from the sunlight streaming in her window that it was midmorning. She could hear Livvy across the hall in her crib, happily gurgling to herself.

She felt like a terrible mother for not being up and taking care of her, for leaving her alone in her crib. She spent enough time alone in her young life. But she was just so tired.

Rolling over, intending to grab her phone, she saw a piece of paper sitting on her nightstand, and before she even picked it up, she knew who it was from and she smiled.

Doyle.

Good morning, Olive.

I don't know if you remember, but you were up to feed the baby once, and then I got up and you told me what to do. You seemed kind of groggy, so I just wanted you to know that the last time Livvy ate was around 4 AM. After I fed her, I checked on you, and then I figured I better go back home.

But first I wanted to write this note, just to let you know what happened last night and also to let you know that I'm planning on picking you up at twelve today. The wedding is at three, and you said you needed to be early. If you need me to pick you up at a different time, let me know. Otherwise, I'll see you then. If you need me to bring you anything, I can do that too. I took care of returning your car, and I know you don't have one now.

Your _friend_,
Doyle.

He had "friend" underlined. Which made her smile. He was letting her know that he was being her friend. He had always been her friend. A far better friend to her than she had been to him.

And that little extra underline, that little extra communication, warmed her heart, because it made her feel like they were talking without words. And that he remembered their earlier conversations. That he cared. That was the thing. She felt like she was with someone who cared. Not that her sisters didn't, because she knew they did.

She'd been plenty of places in the world, alone, by herself, with no one who cared, so being back in Raspberry Ridge, being with Doyle, knowing that he cared, meant a lot to her and gave her the feeling of home like nothing else could.

She guessed that he had left a note because he hadn't wanted to send a text and risk waking her up.

She picked up her phone and pulled up his text.

Twelve is fine. Thank you so much for last night.

She hoped she could be ready by twelve. She didn't have a whole lot of clothes to choose from, so she hoped her clothing choice was okay too.

Now, she just needed the energy to get up and actually get herself ready. Plus, get Livvy ready too. No sooner had she thought that than Livvy's happy gurgles started to sound like fussy whimpers.

It wouldn't be long until those fussy whimpers were full-on loud baby cries, and it would be really nice if she could get out of bed and go to the bathroom at least before she needed to take care of her baby.

Children were so hard.

Or maybe it was just being a single mom that was hard, because last night wasn't so bad. She had someone helping her. For the first time since she left the hospital in Ecuador.

Pulling herself out of bed, feeling like her legs were going to buckle underneath her at any second, panting because it was so much harder than she expected, she did what she needed to do before she went over and tried to muster the strength to pick up her baby. Deciding that it would be best for her to have a bottle made first, she changed course and saw that Doyle had left the formula and a bottle sitting at the top of the stairs.

She could have kissed him right then.

So grateful she didn't have to go downstairs, she almost cried.

She was able to make a bottle and pick up Livvy before she really started to go at it. Immediately when she saw her mom's face, her cries turned to a watery smile.

It was the smile that always did her in. She just couldn't resist it. Her daughter was adorable. If she did have to say so herself.

Thankfully she still had almost three hours, and she was able to feed her baby, get a shower, and get dressed by the time Doyle pulled in, fifteen minutes early.

She couldn't tell how relieved she was. She had never been this exhausted before in her life, and she wondered if it was just a side effect of being sick for so long, or if there was something else going on. Maybe she should take a vitamin.

Whatever was, she didn't want Doyle, or either one of her sisters, to worry about her, and she definitely didn't want to ruin Mertie's big day. She had a feeling that Mertie would only be married one time in her life, and this was her day. She wanted it to be special.

"I wasn't sure if you would be up and ready or not," Doyle said as he gave a perfunctory knock on the door and then stepped in.

It was a relief that she didn't have to get up and go answer it.

"I almost wasn't. I am kind of tired." That was an understatement, but she could live with that. It was true. She was definitely tired.

"I would like it if you could take some time to rest. I think it would benefit both you and Livvy if you could do that." He paused for a moment, and then he said, "You can tell me if I'm pushing too hard, but I'd really like for you to let me take care of you for a few days. I think you'd feel better if you just allowed someone else to do most of the heavy lifting."

"Let's get through today. I'm not going to stay in bed on my sister's wedding day."

It wasn't a yes, and Doyle's flattened lips showed that he knew that, but he nodded.

"Fair enough. Today we celebrate, tomorrow you stay in bed all day."

"Can I sit on the porch?" she asked, knowing she still hadn't agreed but wanting to know how serious he was about not letting her do anything.

"I take care of the baby all day, you do no work. You can sit on the porch, lie on the couch, or stay in bed all day, I don't care. You're just not to do any work. Deal?"

She nodded. Staying in bed all day sounded heavenly right now. Her feet felt like they were so heavy she could barely lift one in front of the other.

"Deal."

"All right. Let's get this show on the road." He laughed a little. "I was going to say the sooner we get out of here, the sooner we can get home, but that's probably not true." She smiled. "Also, Cassie made a sandwich for you." He held up a sandwich wrapped in aluminum foil that he'd been holding in his hand and she'd not noticed.

"I'm so hungry," she said. She had been working on getting herself something to eat. Or at least thinking about it, but she had been so tired, all she'd done was think about the easiest things that she could make, and since they had no cereal, everything else required more than she thought she could handle.

"I think we have enough time for you to go ahead and eat this. I'll trade you," he said, indicating Livvy.

"I think you like her," she said, and maybe she just said that because she wanted to see his reaction. She wanted him to like her.

"She's grown on me. I actually feel like I can relate to her a lot. She likes to eat, and she likes to sleep, and we have all that in common."

Olive laughed. "I have that in common with both of you too."

"What you need to do is sleep." He didn't say anything else, but she got the feeling that he was going to insist that she take it easy for a bit. And she really appreciated that, honestly. She knew she'd been pushing herself too hard and she hadn't been fully recovered from everything she'd gone through. Today, it had really caught up to her.

Too bad the wedding wasn't a different day, because she would gladly stay in bed.

Doyle held the baby, chattering with her, little bits of nonsense that made her laugh and reach for his nose while Olive worked on eating the sandwich. Even eating felt like too much work. And she only made it through half the sandwich.

"I'm full. I don't think I can eat another bite."

"That wasn't very much," he said, looking at the half sandwich and then eyeing her like she might have been hiding something from him. "Are you sure you feel okay?"

"I feel fine."

"I'm going to touch your forehead and see if you have a fever."

She was going to protest, but then she figured it would turn into an argument and she just didn't have the energy. Instead, she leaned forward a little and closed her eyes.

She waited. It took longer than what she expected, and then finally, she felt a featherlike touch along her temple as he moved his finger up across her skin. It was a gentle touch, light and easy and exactly what she needed. It rested her weary soul somehow, like the gentle stroke was all her exhausted body could handle.

He allowed three fingers to rest on her forehead for just a few seconds, and then his light touch went down the other side, to her temple, touching her hair for just a second before he moved his hand away.

It took her a few long moments before she opened her eyes.

"No fever," he said softly.

She swallowed, wondering if she would be able to find her voice. "I didn't think I was sick. I honestly am just tired; I admit, very tired."

"Well, we'll see what we can do about leaving early, although I understand it's your sister's wedding, and it's not like today is going to come around again. So, I know you want to enjoy it."

"I totally forgot about bringing anything to eat. Oh, I'm the worst sister in the world," she said, putting an elbow on the table and dropping her head into her hands. How could she have not remembered that she was supposed to make something? All the guests were supposed to bring something to share.

"I have us covered. I asked Cassie to make something. She's pushy and makes me uncomfortable, but she's an excellent cook. She actually made two dishes, her Parmesan-crusted carrots, which I think are my favorite of everything that she makes, and then a casserole that I'm not exactly sure what's in it, but it smells really good. She's borrowing Fran's car and bringing them."

"You're amazing. I really appreciate it. I...totally dropped the ball."

"Give yourself some grace. You deserve it. You can't be on all the time, especially when you just got back, and you were sick."

"But I've spent a decade ignoring my family, living for myself. And here I am back and I'm still not doing what I want to do."

"But you're working on it. And you did something pretty amazing with Cassie. She's backed off completely on me, and I think she's thinking about what you said because she asked me a couple questions about what the Bible said about different things, mostly the blood sacrifice and why Jesus was qualified to make it. She wasn't sure she believed that he was God's son."

"Wow. If she is questioning things, she's thinking. That's really exciting." She lifted her head up and felt her heart lighten, even if her body still felt heavy.

"I thought you were nuts for walking away from her the way you did and leaving because she asked you to, but you definitely left the door wide open for her to draw closer to Jesus. It was a sacrifice on your part, and while I know God convicts people and draws them to Him, we can help that process along, or we can hinder it. I'm ashamed to admit that probably more than I'd like to, I've hindered it, because I haven't shown Jesus the way I should have."

"Same for me," she said simply, because it was true.

"Are you ready to go?" she said, realizing that it was twelve o'clock, and they hadn't left. She should be early, in plenty of time, but she didn't want to be late for Mertie's wedding. It was a huge celebration, and she was so happy for her sister.

"I'll put Livvy in her car seat. Do you have anything else you need to bring?"

"Just a baby bag, which I have packed. And by the way, thanks for letting that formula and bottle sit at the top of the steps. It was a godsend this morning." Maybe someday she'd tell him exactly how exhausted she was, but she didn't think right now was the right time. She didn't want him to decide that she needed to stay in bed after all.

"Glad you saw it. I almost put it in the note, but I was running out of room on that piece of paper."

"I appreciated the note too."

They smiled, and then she pushed herself out of the chair and they walked out of the house, heading toward her sister's wedding.

Nineteen

"**A**re you sure about this?" Mertie asked as she looked up at the man who was going to pledge his life to her in less than thirty minutes.

"Of course. I've never been more sure about anything. There is no doubt in my mind that God worked out our love story."

"But I'm bossy. And I try to control things and people. And I might end up saying something that's going to cause problems in the church. I might not be a very good pastor's wife."

"You're going to be a perfect pastor's wife. And I know your faults. I'm not blind. But I also know that you don't want to have those faults, and you're working on them. And if I say, 'hey, Mertie, maybe you're being a little bit bossy right now,' you're going to know exactly what I mean and you're going to want to try to fix it. I would rather have that than someone who sits in the corner and never says anything."

"That's not going to be me," she said, irony in her words. She'd never been able to sit in a corner and allow things to go on around her without wanting to fix them and make them better. It was just part of her personality. Her sister, Olive, on the other hand, might sit in a corner and daydream and never pay any attention to anything that was going on.

But Garnet said that he didn't want someone like Olive.

"Are you really going to be able to put up with me?" she asked, even though she knew what his answer was going to be. She just couldn't believe that...

"Are you having trouble believing that someone could love you?" he asked, running his fingers over her cheek and through her hair, pulling her close to him, and wrapping his arms around her. "I can't even tell you how much I love you. It's a feeling, true, but it's a feeling that makes me want to do everything I can to make your life as easy as possible. Which brings me to my concern, which is...are you sure you're okay with being a pastor's wife? This last week, where I got called to the hospital five times, and had to deal with a couple who were having an issue with their son, and with all of the other things that were pulling my attention, and we only have a small church. I'm afraid that sometimes you're going to feel neglected. Sometimes it's going to be hard, and I know it's going to be painful at times. People can be harsh, and they expect the pastor's wife to be perfect. The pastor's family to be perfect. I mean, I love the people in our church, I think they're awesome, but they're human just like me and you."

"I know. I've been in the industry long enough to know that Christians can sometimes be some of the harshest, meanest people on the planet. I've been hurt by them before, and I'm sure that my times of being hurt are not over."

"That bothers me more than anything. I feel like I'm pulling you into something that is going to be painful, and I wish that there was something I could do to make it so that it was easy for you."

"I don't want easy." She tried to make her words as forceful as possible so that he understood she knew exactly what she was saying and she meant it. "I mean, everyone would choose easy if they could, right? But I know that easy isn't going to make me better. It's only when I go through the trials that God has planned for me, and not a single trial is going to come into my life without God okaying it, and that's how I grow. That's how I become better. And I do want to become better."

"That's one of the many things I love about you. That you do want to grow and be better. That you think about things and don't just have a knee-jerk reaction, being ideological and no one can reason with you.

You're willing to look at the bigger picture and see that you might possibly be wrong. I just hope I can do that as well as you do. You're a really good example to me that way."

"You've been a good example to me in a lot of ways. Your sacrifice. That's probably the biggest one. You didn't have to keep Dabney, but you sacrificed whatever was necessary in order for you to do that. Being a single dad, homeschooling, trying to raise her around working a full-time job. You are amazing. How could I not love you?" she asked, running her fingers through the hair at his temple and wondering to herself what had made God decide to give her such an amazing, almost perfect man. "I don't deserve you."

"That's not true. You deserve better."

They smiled into each other's eyes. And she figured that it was probably a mark of the start to a really good marriage that neither one of them were thinking that the other was lucky to get them, but instead was thinking that they were blessed to have the other one. She'd seen way too many people who were so cocky and sure about themselves that they thought that they were doing their spouse a favor by marrying them. That their spouse had to earn their favor, earn their good nature, and continue to work to deserve to get to spend their life with them. Those kinds of marriages didn't usually last, and they weren't good for either party.

"I wish I could have given you a bigger wedding, more flowers, more guests, more everything."

She shook her head. "I don't want that. I don't want the big show, big pomp and circumstance. I understand it's a big day, but to try to make this day all about my fairy-tale dreams coming true is not just selfish, but foolish. It's a waste of money, and it's dragging people, mostly you, through a lot of decisions and difficulties when the wedding doesn't have to be nearly that hard."

"You deserve every good thing."

"God will give me everything that I deserve, I'm sure of it. In the meantime, I love that you're having Pastor Calvin marry us. That's perfectly right. The baton being passed from one pastor to the next, and he was our pastor growing up. It's just...perfect. And while he probably could have made it to the church, it's so nice to do it here for him and be considerate of Mrs. Calvin and him."

"I'm glad you see that."

"It was just so much more low-key, so much friendlier to be able to say to the congregation, come if you want to. Bring food if you want to. Celebrate with us if you want to. No pressure."

"No invitations to have to deal with, no caterer, no last-minute deliveries, no panic because something didn't turn out right. But I would have liked to see you in a beautiful wedding dress."

Had he meant that? Did he want that just because he thought that's what she wanted? Or had he really wanted to see her all dressed up?

"For you or for me?" she asked, tilting her head.

"For you. Doesn't every girl want to dress up in a pretty dress?"

"I think it would look out of place in the assisted living center. I think this is perfect." She indicated the dress she was wearing. It was white with a shimmering gauze over it with blue flowers. Not a wedding dress by any stretch, but a pretty dress that made her feel beautiful and girlish, while still being solemn enough for the occasion.

"You look beautiful in anything."

"Are these the kind of compliments I can expect for the rest of my life? Things that are blatantly not true?" she teased him.

"It's absolutely true. When I look at you, I see beautiful. I know that's probably not what you always see, but that's just what I see when I look at you."

She lifted her head up and kissed his cheek, and then he turned his head and their lips met. Maybe they shouldn't have been kissing before the wedding, wasn't there some kind of saying that said it was bad luck for them to see each other before they were married, but she didn't believe in luck. She believed in God, and she believed that God had an amazing plan for the rest of their life together. She also believed that there was nothing wrong with kissing. In fact, it was very, very nice.

"Are you two ready?" Amara knocked on the door and then stuck her head in. "Oh! I'm sorry."

They broke apart, just far enough so that they could look into each other's eyes but not lose the connection of touching between them.

"You don't have to apologize," Mertie said.

"And we're ready," Garnet added without breaking the connection they shared both physical and with their eyes.

Mertie couldn't say she wasn't the slightest bit nervous, but she did know that what she was doing was the smartest thing she could possibly do. She also knew for sure that it was God's will, and that is what made it okay.

"Dabney's outside waiting to walk up the aisle," Amara said.

"All right. We'll be there," Garnet replied.

"Thank you. Thank you for taking care of my daughter for so long and for believing in me. Not that I was a good Christian speaker-author or whatever. But believing that I would be a good mom." If it hadn't been for Garnet's belief in her, this day would not be possible.

"I just believe in what I see. And it's all there."

He couldn't possibly see her. He had to see Jesus somehow, and that made her smile. She reached up, kissing the bottom of his jaw, and then moved back until they clasped hands. "Let's do this," she said.

"I'm with you," he replied, and they walked out the door. Toward the rest of their life.

Twenty

The gathering room of the assisted living facility was packed to the brim. Pretty much every person who lived there had to have come to see the big day. Olive doubted that many weddings took place here.

Plus, every person that she'd ever seen at the church in her life was also in attendance. Or at least it seemed like that. She couldn't think of a single person she knew who wasn't there.

"That's a lot of people," Doyle whispered from behind her, leaning down so he could reach her ear and speak softly.

"Cassie even made it. I'm glad."

"She was making food for it. Not just for us, but she wanted to bring some for herself. She really enjoys cooking."

"Everything she makes is delicious," Olive said, wanting to give her the credit that was her due. Even though she still wasn't sure what exactly had gone on between Doyle and her. Doyle claimed it was nothing, other than Cassie wanting to be with him, and she had to believe him. He had not lied to her before, and she hoped that this was not the one time he made an exception. In fact, she wouldn't allow her head to go there. It wasn't right. It would just undermine their relationship.

What was in the past was done and over with, and she needed to focus on the future, although she appreciated knowing about the past, so she was prepared for any meetings or confrontations she might have.

Of course, she'd been burned once before, with Ricardo. She wasn't even sure what she saw in him, other than maybe she was just lonely. That was the only excuse she could think of to explain her behavior.

A guitar started to play, and Olive craned her head trying to see who it was.

"I think it's that family up the road from Raspberry Ridge who has all the children who sometimes go round to festivals to sing. The Carter family?"

"I knew there were benefits to being with someone who was so tall," Olive teased.

Doyle put his free hand on her shoulder and squeezed. "I'm glad I'm of some use to you."

"You're holding my baby too," she said easily.

It was standing room only, and the room was warm. She truly was grateful that he was holding the baby, because she already felt faint. She could hardly take a chair when there were several ladies who were twice her age standing. But she wanted to, since she felt like she was going to fall over at any moment. Or more likely her knees were going to buckle.

"How are you doing?" Doyle asked, his lips brushing the hair beside her temple as he spoke.

She suppressed a shiver and closed her eyes to enjoy it. He couldn't see her face, and even if he could, he might think she was just tired.

"I'm fine." It was all she could say. What was she supposed to say other than complain? Tell him that she needed to go sit down? But she couldn't do it in front of the older ladies, and she couldn't take a seat that one of them might be able to use. So she just had to deal with it. It would be over soon, and while she didn't want to rush it because it was the only wedding her sister would ever have, she did want to try to endure.

"You'll let me know if you think you need to leave?"

"I will. But I won't have to. I'm going to stand and I'm going to watch this and I'm going to celebrate with her because this is a fantastic day for her. Maybe the best day of her life."

"I have to say, it's the best wedding I've ever been to."

"And probably the one with the least amount of work put into it," Olive added, thinking that Mertie had been extremely smart to do things the way she had. No fuss, no stress, just people who wanted to be there and celebrate with them.

There would be a bit of an extra mess to clean up, but Mertie had told her that the assisted living center was going to take care of it and she was giving them a bit of money to pay any overtime their staff might need.

The crowd gasped, and Olive turned again, able to peek through the heads and see that Dabney had started walking up the aisle between two groups of chairs.

She was beautiful, with her hair piled high and the long seafoam green dress she wore swirling about her ankles. She looked so grown up. And yet vulnerable and young at the same time. Definitely she also looked happy, and why wouldn't she be? Her parents were getting married.

She made it to the front, where Garnet already stood, waiting. He must have walked up the side and she missed it, since he hadn't been there earlier when she checked. Regardless, father and daughter shared a sweet smile, tender and gentle and yet full of excitement and hope.

It made Olive's chest feel light and happy. A family was being created today, one that was going to stand for Jesus and live for him. It scared her a bit, because she knew those were the kinds of families the devil attacked the most stridently, but she had faith that God would protect them and that her sister and her husband would stay true to the end and that they'd hear that coveted "well done."

It was what she wanted to hear at the end of her life as well.

Then the folks sitting in the chairs froze as the tune on the guitar changed from a romantic melody to more of a march-type piece. Not the wedding march but something close.

More gasps as the crowd murmured and shifted, and Olive was finally able to get a glimpse of her sister walking slowly up the aisle, her eyes on her groom.

Their dad had died in a car accident, and she didn't have anyone to walk her up, but she clutched a single blue carnation in front of her and didn't seem bothered by the fact that she was alone.

Her eyes shone, and Olive didn't think she'd ever seen her sister look more beautiful. There were some camera flashes, and Doyle said, "I'd heard that they were trying to keep the paparazzi out, and that was part of the reason that they were doing this quietly and low-key. Because of Mertie's national platform and the fact that a lot of people would like to see her get married."

"That's what I heard too. The local police are supposed to be standing in the parking lot and keeping an eye out for people they don't know." Which had made Olive laugh. That was how the locals kept security. There were no invitations or badges to show. The police just had to recognize them.

They had gotten there before the police had set up their checking stations, so she didn't know whether it was true or not, but the idea made her smile.

Mertie had confided in both her and Amara that she didn't really care if people took pictures of her, since it didn't matter. She just didn't want the place to be overrun with cameras and press and have big stories in national newspapers about anything that might have happened. So they were just going to make an effort but not get legalistic about it.

It seemed like a good way to go. Do what you could, and roll with the rest. Maybe that was a good way to live life, to not get stressed and anxious, but you just do what you could, trust the Lord, and roll with the rest.

Pastor Calvin now stood beside Garnet as Mertie made her way to the front. The wedding was short and sweet, with the pastor giving a few words about marriage and what it meant, and a little advice on how to have a good marriage. He used the golden rule, which Olive figured was probably a good rule for any relationship, including marriage.

How could a marriage fail if both of the parties were trying their hardest to treat the other person the way they wanted to be treated?

The pastor mentioned that it was important to obey the golden rule no matter how the other person treated you. Olive couldn't agree more, but she knew how hard that was. It wasn't easy to be nice to someone who wasn't being nice to you.

"You showed that really well with Cassie," Doyle whispered in her ear. "He could use you as an example."

She shook her head but didn't answer him, and he couldn't see the smile that his words had put on her face. She appreciated the fact that he noticed and complimented her and admired that. It was something she had done quietly, without fanfare, without drawing attention to herself, but it was still nice to get a little credit for it. Especially from Doyle; somehow that made it even better.

His words helped her take her mind off of the way her knees had started trembling and the way she felt like she couldn't get enough air. It felt so hot, and she was so tired, and it was already so hard for her to hold herself up, since she felt so heavy.

"May I present to you Mr. and Mrs. Garnet Irving. You may kiss your bride." Pastor Calvin beamed at the couple as they glanced at him, then at each other, and Garnet leaned down for a short, sweet kiss as the crowd cheered and clapped.

Garnet straightened, and Mertie smiled, and Olive's heart swelled. So happy for her sister and hoping that someday, maybe she would have the same good fortune, God would smile on her and give her a man who was as honorable and upright as Garnet was.

Of course, she had an honorable and upright man standing behind her, but she'd hurt him terribly, and maybe God would not give her a second chance.

She'd no sooner thought that, as she smiled weakly, than everything around her went black.

Twenty-One

"What do you think, Doc?" Doyle said, trying to keep the panic out of his voice.

When Olive had collapsed in front of him, he almost hadn't caught her. Thankfully his hand, the one that hadn't been holding Livvy, had been on her shoulder, and he felt her start to fall. He'd been able to wrap his hand around her waist and keep her from hitting the ground, but then he'd had to get someone to hold the baby while he put both arms around Olive and carried her to a cooler room where she had more room to breathe.

Thankfully the wedding was in the assisted care facility, and there happened to be a doctor in the building.

He'd come as soon as he had been called, and Doyle had told him Olive's history of having a baby and having malaria and how she'd been tired and weak lately.

"I think you're right. I think it's mostly fatigue. She has no fever, and her heartbeat and respiration are steady, her oxygen stats and blood pressure are all good. Still, she should probably go to her doctor and be checked out, but in the absence of any other symptoms, I recommend a lot of rest, as well as a follow-up visit to someone else who can run the tests that I cannot."

He shifted Livvy who was back in his arms. He didn't even know who had held her while he'd carried Olive.

Olive blinked, but she hadn't said much since she'd regained consciousness, shortly after he'd set her down.

"Thanks, Doc." He paused, then said, "How much do I owe you?"

The doc waved his hand. "I'm here on call. I'm being paid whether I see people or not. This was a little extra, a nice break in my routine." He put a hand on Olive's shoulder. "I hope you feel better, miss."

Mertie had been extremely concerned, but Doyle had convinced them to take the wedding party and continue to the cafeteria where they were all going to eat. He told her that he didn't think that there was anything seriously wrong, but he would let her know as soon as he knew.

"I'm typing a text to your sister letting her know exactly what the doctor said. I told her I would." It wasn't easy to type a text with one hand while he held the baby in the other, but he was getting rather good at it. In fact, he kind of liked the way the baby felt in his arms, her chubby warmth and her sweet smiles. Of course, there were other things less lovely, like dirty diapers and middle of the night crying, but she was a sweetheart, and he found himself falling in love with her.

"I feel terrible that I took so much attention away from the bride and groom. That wasn't my intention at all."

"And they know that. It's not like someone chooses to pass out at a wedding. Plus, you were considerate enough to wait until they presented the bride and groom and people saw them kiss and cheered for them."

Her eyes closed wearily, and it seemed like her whole body fell into itself as she breathed out.

He felt better now that the doctor had taken her blood pressure, which had been low but still in the normal range, and taken the other stats as well. Still, he wanted her to go see a doctor.

"Do you want to make that appointment, or do you want me to do it for you?" he asked, figuring that maybe that question would be better than asking her if she was going to do it.

"What appointment?" she asked, her eyes barely opening before they shut again like her eyelids were too heavy for her to hold open.

"For you to see the doctor. He said he couldn't see anything wrong, but he recommended rest and another doctor's appointment. I can make it if you're too tired to."

"I can't afford it just now. I know it's just that I'm tired. Just need to rest."

"I think you're probably right. After all, you've been through a lot, but I think it would be better to be safe than sorry. I'll pay for it—" He put his hand up as she started to interrupt him. "And you can pay me back. But it would make me feel better if you got checked."

"I don't think I need a doctor," she said, her lips set in a stubborn line even though her eyes were still closed.

"I think Livvy deserves to have a mother who can raise her and doesn't die of some disease that could have been caught and cured if the mother hadn't been too stubborn to go to the doctor. Now I think that you're right, that you're just tired, but I also think that you need to get checked out."

He brought Livvy into the conversation because he thought that that might sway Olive, and he'd been right. As soon as he said Livvy's name, her eyes opened and landed on her baby, and a soft, maternal look came over her face. Her mulish expression melted into acquiescence by the time he finished speaking.

"Do you mind?" she said wearily. "The very idea of calling and trying to figure it out and then going, and then they'll probably want to send me for tests, and I just... I don't think I can do it all."

"I will take care of it for you."

"I don't have a doctor."

"That's fine. Blueberry Beach has a new hospital, and I'm sure there are doctors there who are accepting new patients. We'll get you in with someone."

"I'm sorry to be such a problem."

"You're not a problem. I actually feel like I'm doing something taking care of you. It doesn't necessarily give me a purpose exactly, I just...like it," he finished lamely. Unable to articulate exactly how he felt about it. He wanted to take care of her. He wanted to protect her and provide for her and be the person that she could depend on for whatever she needed. It was an honor to be able to call the doctor and make the appointment and watch her baby and do all the things.

Last time you got too involved with her, she cut her losses and cut out, leaving you with a broken heart.

He heard that voice in his head, and he had to give it credence because it was correct.

But she's changed. She's not the same person that she was, and she's not going to do that again.

You don't know that. The only thing you have to go on is her word.

Her behavior is different, I've seen it. Look at what she did for Cassie.

The voice was silent. It was true that he didn't know anyone else who would do what Olive had done, who would be more concerned about the person's salvation than they were about getting their own way, or winning an argument, or giving up what they had every right to.

And yet wasn't that the example that Jesus sent? He had given up his throne in heaven, given up the access that he had to ten thousand angels who could have come and saved him from the crowds who wanted to crucify him. And yet, he allowed them to do it, not just because he had the sins of the world to pay for, but because allowing them to crucify him, rather than killing them and keeping them from it, meant that perhaps they would see what he had done, believe in him, and be saved from an eternity in hell.

He'd never seen such a living example of what Jesus had done, even though what Olive did was just a shadow of his sacrifice. He still felt like she was on the right track.

And if that was the kind of person that she'd become after rededicating her life to the Lord, he knew that he could trust his heart with her.

Of course, he didn't know how she felt about him.

"I'd like to take you home, but I'm guessing that you'd like to stay and be a part of your sister's wedding if possible."

"I was wondering how I was going to say that to you. I know I just passed out, and I don't want to cause any more problems for anyone or take any more attention off of Mertie, but I would like to stay, at least until people have eaten and all the celebration is mostly over." She paused, and then she said, "But if it's going to be too much trouble, and you're afraid that you might have to do more than just carry me to the car, I'm willing to leave. If that's best for you."

It would have been best for him. It would take a lot of the worry off his shoulders and keep him from spending the next two hours wondering if he was going to catch her if she passed out. But he couldn't say that to her, because he didn't want her to miss the celebration of her sister's wedding. He knew how much it meant to her.

"Let's stay. But only if you promise to let me know the next time you're feeling the way you felt before you passed out."

"I promise."

"How about we just try sitting you up a little bit first, okay?"

She nodded, and he said, "Let me set Livvy down. She's going to need to be changed and have a bottle soon. I didn't keep track of the last time I gave her one, but I know it's been a while."

"I think you're right. I'm sorry. You're doing everything."

"Stop apologizing, it's not necessary. I wouldn't be here if I didn't want to be. You have lots of other people who would love to help take care of you, and I'm the one who gets that honor, and that's what it is. An honor."

She gave him a look like she didn't believe what he was saying, but she didn't argue. Probably because she didn't have the energy, and he almost made a crack about how nice it was when she was too tired to argue, but he didn't.

She sat up and swayed a little, like she was still a bit dizzy. He knew it would be best to take her straight home, but he'd help her as long as he could. Because it was what she wanted and he found he couldn't tell her no.

Twenty-Two

"I think Cassie should start a restaurant," Amara said as she sat at the table with Olive and Doyle. Hobert had gone to fill up her drink.

"She definitely makes delicious food. And she really seems to enjoy it," Olive said, hoping that she didn't sound as tired as she felt. She knew, after passing out, that she would probably be paying for all of this tomorrow, but she really wanted to stay and enjoy her sister's wedding. Doyle had been phenomenal, taking care of Livvy, making sure that she had whatever she needed on her plate, and anticipating her needs before she even knew what they were. He had been amazing, and more than one time, she had thought to herself that she had given him up out of her stupidity.

And wished that there was going to be a second chance for her.

"Are you sure you're okay? You look so tired. I don't want to keep bringing it up in case you're trying to forget about it, but I just want you to know that I'm a little bit worried." Amara leaned toward her and spoke softly, as though she didn't want to throw all of her cares and concerns out into the open.

"I'm tired. I'm not going to lie. But Doyle has been amazing; I wouldn't be here without him, but I'm glad that I am, because I don't want to miss Mertie's wedding. I'm assuming she's not going to have another."

"I think that's what we all would like to hear. For her, as well as ourselves."

"Are you still getting married next week?"

Amara grinned as Hobert came back, carrying her glass. "We're hoping to. We weren't planning on having it at the assisted living facility here, although I kind of feel like this was a good choice. There is lots of room, lots of friendly people, and the folks who live here are having a blast."

"I doubt they've ever had a wedding in their facility before."

"I have to agree," Amara said, smiling her thanks at Hobert who handed her a frosty cold glass of water. "And I think they're having the time of their lives."

"I can't believe some of these people are dancing," Olive said, wishing she had the energy to get up and dance.

"Speaking of dancing, would you be interested?" Hobert asked, holding a hand out for Amara as a slow, sensual song came on.

"I would love to," Amara said, and Olive doubted that anything had ever been more true.

She stood up, and they held hands as they walked out to the area that they cleared off in the cafeteria to double as the dance floor.

The place still smelled like mashed potatoes and a little musty, but the happy atmosphere, the smiling faces, and the camaraderie that seemed to permeate the entire building made any smells feel happy and add to the celebration, rather than detract from it.

"Are you up for dancing?" Doyle asked from beside her.

She glanced at the table where Livvy's car seat sat with Livvy sleeping inside. That was another good thing about being at the assisted living facility. No one was going to take her baby. And she really, really wanted to dance with Doyle.

"I am," she said, putting her hand in his, and while she didn't exactly jump to her feet, she rose slowly, fighting the waves of fatigue and dizziness.

"I think we could just dance right here, if that's okay with you," Doyle said, pulling her slightly so that she stepped into his arms, and he put his arm around her, pressing her to him, and while it felt good to be so close, he also helped steady her and hold her on her feet, which made her feel even better.

They didn't move fast but just swayed from side to side, which was perfect for her. She could lean into his strength and enjoy the music and the dance without putting too much effort out at all.

She felt a little like maybe she was cheating, but being in Doyle's arms made everything worthwhile.

"I wouldn't have had this day without you. I just wanted to thank you."

"And here I thought it should be me thanking you for giving me one of the best days of my life. Other than that scare when you fell."

"Sorry about that, although, is this really one of the best days of your life?"

"I held you more today than I ever have before. That makes it a good day."

He smiled down at her, and she kind of thought that maybe he was teasing a bit. She wanted to laugh, but if he was being serious, she didn't want to brush it off, because she appreciated the way he'd been treating her.

"I hope it's okay, but I told Cassie about your sister." That was a total change of subject, but she'd been meaning to admit to him that she had, just in case Cassie said something.

"Thanks for telling me. I don't think I ever mentioned it to her, although I believe she was my housekeeper when the accident happened."

"That's what I thought too, and I told her so, but I figured that it was probably just something you didn't want to talk about. I know the two of you were close."

"We were. Especially since my parents seem so distant."

"She said they moved to Canada?" She wanted to know everything there was to know about him.

"They did. I hear from them at Christmas, get a card. A halfhearted invitation to join them, when they'd be shocked if I said yes and more than a little bit put out."

She laughed. "It's very similar to my parents, only mine, instead of moving to a different country, they just kind of immersed themselves into their business. At times, it seemed like they even forgot that they had children."

"Yeah, I remember they didn't really pay attention to you, even when you lived in Raspberry Ridge." He paused for a moment, as they swayed gently to the music, and then he said, "Why did you come back that summer?"

She hesitated, thinking back, knowing the answer that came to her mind immediately, but not wanting to say it if it wasn't true.

"You don't have to tell me if you don't want to."

"It's not that I don't want to. I just wanted to make sure I was saying the truth."

"Well, thank you. I appreciate that. I wouldn't want you to lie to me."

"After being lied to by Ricardo, where he had a wife and kids on the side, and he didn't bother to tell me, he acted like they didn't exist, I've been very sensitive to lying. It...hurt at the time, but it cured me, because I had a tendency to tell little fibs that made things easier. Whether it was giving someone a compliment that I didn't really mean or putting my sisters off by telling them I couldn't get airplane tickets or something, you know?"

"Yeah. I guess that was never really something that I had a problem with, but I can understand how an experience like you went through would make you feel like you never wanted to do that again, after the way it hurt you."

"It's funny how our experiences do that to us. Finally opens our eyes to things that we hadn't realized or known."

"It makes me wonder what all there is that I really don't know. You know? If our experiences open our eyes, there's lots of things I haven't experienced. What don't I know?"

"That's such a great point, and I've never thought of that before." She was a little out of breath, but she didn't want to stop talking. Doyle had always been an interesting conversationalist, talking about far more than just the weather or whatever people talked about when they did small talk. His conversations were deeper and more interesting. They often talked about ideas, and dreams and hopes, which were far more interesting to her than the weather. Which they couldn't do anything about anyway.

"I guess over the years as I thought about that, it's made me more sensitive or compassionate to people. They have experiences that I don't, and I don't want to dismiss that. Although, my experiences have shaped me as well. So there's value in both sides."

"That's why it's a good idea to read widely and talk to people from a lot of different walks of life."

"It really shaped you as a person." He laughed a little. "Even though I just want to stay here and live in Raspberry Ridge for the rest of my life. I suppose those two ideas contradict themselves, but you can read a book just as well in Raspberry Ridge as you can anywhere else."

"That's true, you can. And books definitely give you a slice of life that you might not have if you stay where you are and don't read."

"TV fits the bill a little bit, but not nearly as much, because even real-life shows are scripted."

"Documentaries are great for information, but they don't really give you the human side of things."

The song ended, and people politely clapped. Olive didn't let go of Doyle, and it was only partially because she thought she might get dizzy and fall again. It was mostly because holding onto him felt good and made her feel supported in a way that she hadn't in a very long time, if ever.

"You know, you never answered my question," Doyle said as another song came on, this one a little faster, but neither one of them moved, neither one of them stopped swaying, and they just kind of danced a little like that right beside their table and her sleeping baby.

"Which question?" she asked, wishing that her mind didn't feel like such a mud puddle of mixed-up thoughts and snippets of intelligence that she could hardly see.

"Why did you come back that summer?"

"It was because of you." She looked up at him, wanting to meet his eyes, for him to know that it was the truth.

He still snorted. "I don't believe that."

"It's true. We'd been good friends when I moved away. We'd even written a few letters to each other."

"I remember. Junior high especially, I guess when I started noticing girls, you were the one that always came to my mind."

"And you were the one that always came to mine. I wanted to travel, I wanted to get away, I think now it was just searching for a home, even though I used it as an excuse. Regardless, I wanted to see you. I... compared every other guy I'd ever been with to you."

"And were there a lot of those?" he asked, and then he wrinkled his nose. "I know that's prying, but..."

"No. You have every right to ask. And you can ask whatever you want. I'll answer if I can. But no. There weren't a lot of guys. I was more interested in learning about different countries, and each one I looked at, I tried to think of how it would feel like to live there. I was searching for a home. Anyway, guys came and went, but there was no one serious, no one that I really went out with, other than a few dances here and there that I didn't really enjoy. I'm not sure why. Maybe because they weren't you."

"I think she's telling me that just to make me feel better."

"No. I'm being honest." She lifted her shoulder, unable to force him to believe her, although it was true.

"I couldn't believe it when I saw you. It was right at the beginning of June, and you stayed the whole summer."

"There was an apartment above Fran's store that was open at the time, and she rented it to me. Probably cheaper than she should have, since she knew me, and I think she was happy to have me back."

"I can see how she feels. I was so thrilled that you were back, I couldn't believe it. And you'd grown up to be so beautiful."

"You were everything that I had imagined, only taller."

"I kind of shot up there about the time I was sixteen or so. I didn't think I was going to stop growing. I kind of had nightmares about it."

"That's funny. I thought every guy wanted to be tall."

"I think there's a balance. You want to be tall, but you don't want to be a toothpick. And tall guys have a tendency to be skinny. But I just didn't stop growing. I didn't want to be twice as high as whatever girl would finally look at me."

"Well, you're not twice as tall as me. And I suppose I'm the girl in front of you now."

"You were the girl in front of me then too. You are beautiful. And you looked at me like you really liked me." He looked over her shoulder, almost as though he couldn't explain how she looked at him, but she remembered. He had been her friend, a good friend, maybe not her best friend exactly but her best friend in Raspberry Ridge. And she was so proud of how he had turned out. Not like he had anything to do with how he looked, but he was planning on doing an internship in the fall. It was different than most of the other kids who were just blindly going off to college like everyone else did, but he had plans that he had made himself, things he had thought about, and a way of doing things that didn't involve following the crowd.

"I admired so much about you. More than your physical height, just the way you had decided to live your life deliberately, not following what everyone else did, but thinking about what your goals were, what you wanted, and doing that."

"I was willing to give it all up, if you would have stayed." He seemed doubtful again.

It was funny how she barely noticed the people around them, the way one song changed into another, but it didn't really affect what they were doing. They just stood beside the table swaying, and she supposed the fact that she had already passed out once made it so the people weren't looking at them oddly, like there was something wrong with them for not even dancing to the beat of the music, just happy in each other's arms.

But that explained her whole relationship with Doyle. She had just always been happy in his arms. Happy beside him, happy with him.

"I wouldn't have wanted you to give that up for me. I would have felt bad about it."

"I would have been happy. Happy to do it, happy to be with you."

"I don't understand what you saw in me."

"Looking back, I've wondered about that too. Not because of anything that I think was wrong with me, just...you're so much better now than you were then. But maybe I've changed too."

"You have. You're mature, you've lived a lot, and back then you knew what you wanted, but I get that same impression from you now.

Your confidence and your knowledge that you are living your life on purpose."

"Isn't that something that most people don't do? Life happens to them, and it's almost like they're reacting to the things that happen, rather than deliberately making a plan and trying to implement that plan, even if it's something as simple as wanting to show Jesus to the people that they meet. That can be a great goal, but then you have to deliberately implement that."

"By reading your Bible, praying, having a relationship with Him, but then you have to apply what you know to your life. I think that's where I get tripped up the most. I know it, but I can't always do it."

"Through the power of the Holy Spirit. Sometimes we rely on ourselves too much. We just need to lift our fingers up and let go."

The upbeat song faded into a slower one, and someone dimmed the lights. Out of the corner of her eye, Olive could see Mertie and Garnet dancing while smiling into each other's eyes and talking together.

She knew that Garnet had some things he needed to do, people who needed him, counsel he had to give, and they would be leaving, going back to their regular life and doing that, not even taking a honeymoon. But they had both said that they felt that the ministry was more important. They did plan a trip later with Dabney going along, because Mertie had told Olive that she felt it was important that they did things as a family together. Even though Dabney had seemed to accept her without too much trouble, she felt that the more things they did together as a family, the more it would give them time to bond.

"So did you really come back to Raspberry Ridge just for me?"

"I did."

"Why did you leave?" he asked, and it was the closest that he'd come to broaching the subject that neither one of them had really talked about. The way she'd left, the way she'd broken his heart, the way he'd offered her everything and she had thrown it all back in his face.

"I guess because I was scared." She looked aside; the weariness had not dissipated, weighing heavy on her chest, but he deserved answers.

"Scared?" he prompted.

She nodded. "You seemed too good to be true. You...treated me well, cared about me, didn't push me to do things that I didn't feel were right, you never tried to take things from me that I didn't want to give. Unlike the guys that I had dated in high school."

His hands tightened on her, and she hurried to say, "I got away from them quickly. It wasn't a matter of me being taken advantage of, I just... appreciated the fact that I didn't always have to be on guard against that, you know?"

He lifted his chin, but his expression remained serious.

"You were everything I wanted. Better than I remembered." She looked away, staring at the dancers but not really seeing them, trying to remember her exact feelings that summer. She wanted to stay, everything that Doyle had offered her was exactly what she'd always wanted, but...

"I guess I was afraid of missing out. I had always wanted to travel, and everyone says, you gotta do it before you're married, or you'll never get it done. And maybe I just listened to that too much. I believed them. I thought it was my only chance to see the world. And I honestly can't even say that I necessarily wanted to do that, definitely no more than I wanted to be with you. But there were all these other voices telling me that I would be making a huge mistake if I got married so young." She took a breath, thinking again about how different that had been from what Doyle had chosen. "You knew exactly what you wanted, and even though everyone else was going to college and taking that well-trodden career path, you did something different. And I admire that. I guess I wish I would have had the ability to say no to the well-trodden path and to take your hand and go with you."

He nodded some but didn't say anything, and she worried a little that maybe there had been something in what she had said that had offended him or made him feel like she had done it once, and she might do it again.

That thought prompted her to say a little more. "I guess after things happened to me in Ecuador, and I was there by myself, sick, with my baby, and all I had was gone, I realized that the well-trodden path isn't always the best path, but more than that, I changed. I determined that I wasn't going to do the easy thing anymore or listen to the voices that tried to tell me that what I knew I should be doing wasn't what I ought to do."

"You did change. You're very different. The same girl, same underlying personality, but the way you live your life is a lot different than it used to be. That's a change I noticed almost right away."

She smiled at his words. Grateful that it hadn't been just a decision that she made, but an actual change that had happened to her.

"I wish it would have happened sooner." Like the summer that she'd been here.

"I don't think we should look back on our lives and wish that we had done things differently. Maybe obvious sin, we can wish away, but... God had a plan. We needed to go through the things we did in order to be where we are today." He gave her a serious look. "As long as you get healthy. Which, I have every intention of making sure that you do."

"You've taken better care of me than my mom ever did. Not that I'm comparing you to my mom. It's different." So much different. And better. Her mom always made it feel like she was an inconvenience if her mom had to take time out of her schedule to take care of her, but Doyle hadn't made her feel like an imposition at all. Even taking care of Livvy seemed like something he enjoyed and not a pain or problem.

Another song ended, and there was clapping, and then the music started again.

"I think that it might be time for you to head home. You seem to be sagging in my arms, and while I don't mind that at all, I'm kind of chomping at the bit to get you in and get you rested, because... I hope that we'll have more days like today."

He seemed a little uncertain in what he had just said, and she wanted to assure him that she had every intention of having lots more days like today, but was it really fair to say that, when he was right. She didn't know what her health was going to be.

"I might never get better." She lifted her brows and said that, voicing her deepest fear out loud. Part of the reason she didn't want to go to the doctor was because she was afraid the doctor would say these were just episodes that she was going to have to deal with since she'd had a complicated version of malaria.

"Then we'll deal with it."

He lifted his brows as though questioning her. They hadn't made any plans for the future, and maybe that's what he was doing, trying to feel her out, see what she thought about it.

But she couldn't agree with him, not when she didn't know whether she could even be a contributing member of society, let alone a contributing member of their marriage.

She couldn't do that.

"I'm ready to go. Let me make my way over to Mertie and congratulate her and give her a hug. And then we can head out."

"We'll go together."

Twenty-Three

Doyle held Olive's arm as they made their way across the cafeteria/dance floor to where Mertie and Garnet were chatting with a few of the older folks in the assisted care facility.

"We were hoping that Pastor Calvin would have a replacement who could do the preaching every Sunday. He has said that it's just a little bit much for him, but there is no one who is willing to come and minister to us. It's not like they get a very big offering." An older lady, her white hair smoothed down into a bob that framed her face, leaned heavily on her walker as she spoke to Pastor Garnet.

Doyle stood back, his arm around Olive. They were finally almost on the way home. He had been waiting for what felt like forever to get her to a place where she could lie down and rest.

"While I can't do it on Sunday morning, obviously, I can definitely take a morning and come and give a lesson. It might be the same message I deliver on Sunday morning, but—"

"We'd appreciate that. In fact, we'd all love that. None of us are going to church in Raspberry Ridge, and so it would be a treat to be able to hear your message."

"I would appreciate having you take over the reins here. Even people who are at the end of their life still need spiritual guidance and exhortation from God's word. It helps with every stage of life, including the end."

"Speak for yourself, pastor. I've got plenty of good years left. I'd say I'm just in the middle of my journey," the woman said, shifting on her walker as she spoke.

Doyle bit back a smile. The woman was feisty and fun, and he could just imagine the merry chase that she led her husband around on, had she been married. There was no ring on her finger at the moment. Although, a woman like that, he would be surprised if she didn't find a husband among the assisted living members.

He hoped he went into his old age like that, determined to stay alive, and not living just with his beating heart and working lungs, but by being engaged with the people around him. Living life that way.

They finished their conversation with Pastor Garnet agreeing to visit the nursing home on Thursday mornings.

"Oh, Mertie. It was a beautiful wedding. Just so perfect. And you are a gorgeous bride," Olive said as she stepped forward, embracing her sister.

"I'm so glad you could come. I'm sorry that I didn't realize how exhausted you were. I would never have dragged you off to Bible study yesterday had I realized."

Olive held her hand up. "No. I wanted to go. You know how it is, you don't want to be sidelined. You want to be in the thick of it. It is hard to admit that maybe you should take a break once in a while."

"Do me a favor, and let Doyle take care of you. He's been pampering you all day, and it's been adorable to watch, but you really should go home and get some real rest." Mertie's eyes shone, but the care she had for her sister was obvious.

"That's where we're heading, but I didn't want to do that without congratulating both of you." Olive stood back and included Pastor Garnet in her words that time.

"Thank you. I have to agree with your assessment. Mertie made a beautiful bride. And the wedding that she put together was the best one I've ever been to. Of course, that might have something to do with me being the groom and getting the most beautiful woman in the room as my bride."

"Garnet," Mertie said.

"I'm not sure I've ever heard you say anything in that tone of voice before," Olive said, smiling at her sister. "I can hardly contain my happiness for you. You guys make the most adorable couple, and I wish you all the best."

"Thank you. You take it easy so you can come to your other sister's wedding next Friday. Lots of changes for your family." Garnet spoke, but above his words, there was a concern in his eyes for his new sister-in-law that Doyle appreciated.

"I'll try to make sure she gets rested up and is there with bells on. My goal will be that she doesn't pass out in the middle of the ceremony again."

"I waited until the end," Olive said to him, batting her lashes, and if he were going to say, he would say that she was flirting with him.

He wanted to call her on it, but instead he said, "I suppose you're right. You did have good timing. I'm sure the happy couple appreciates it."

They all laughed a little, and then Olive allowed him to take her by the waist with one arm, carrying the car seat in the other, as they made their way out of the cafeteria and out of the assisted living facility. Home. That's where they were going. Finally.

Twenty-Four

Olive thought she might go stir-crazy. It had been six days since Mertie's wedding, and Doyle had insisted that she spend most of all of those six days in bed.

She had agreed to it, mostly, because she did want to be better for Amara's wedding which was tomorrow. But other than him allowing her to get out of bed twice each day to go for a walk, right beside him in case she fell, she hadn't gotten out at all.

She did not hold that against Doyle whatsoever. In fact, she appreciated the fact that he had brought all of his work things and spent a good part of each day either outside of her room or downstairs working, taking care of the baby, and making sure that she had nourishing meals.

Most of those meals had been provided by Cassie, who had even delivered a few.

She wouldn't say that she and Cassie were exactly on the greatest terms, but she was still trying to be a friend to her. She thought that perhaps Cassie resented the fact that when Olive left like she'd asked, Doyle had moved out too.

That was not Olive's problem, though. She didn't ask for it, and she

166

wasn't going to ask him to leave her, especially after the care and concern he'd shown her the last few days.

Maybe it was just a matter of the patient falling in love with their caretaker, but she thought that she might be developing feelings for Doyle, if she hadn't already had them.

She wasn't quite sure how to broach the subject though, since he hadn't the entire week that he'd been taking care of her.

Although he had held her in his arms at the wedding and seemed to want to keep her there. But that might have been because he was trying to make sure that she did what he wanted her to.

"How are you doing this afternoon?" Doyle said as he peeked his head in her open door.

"Ready to get out of bed," she said, trying not to sound like she was whining or complaining, but truly tired of staring at the four walls. He had taken her down and allowed her to sit and enjoy the view of Lake Michigan, and she'd spent a little bit of time in the living room, but not nearly enough.

"We have some company, and if you don't mind, I have a proposition for you."

"A proposition?" For her? Is that what he meant?

"For the three of you," Doyle said as he walked in the room followed by Amara and Mertie.

"So that's why you invited us here," Amara said, narrowing her eyes at Doyle before hurrying to Olive's side and giving her a hug.

Olive pushed herself up in bed, swimming through the dizziness that almost always occurred as she sat up. The doctor had said that it would eventually go away, once she got a little stronger. But all of her tests had come back negative, other than the test showing that she had had malaria, but it was inactive.

"Sweetie. Your cheeks are rosy, and you have some color back. That makes me happy," Mertie said, giving her a hug from the other side of the bed. Both her sisters pulled chairs next to her, and each of them held her hand.

"I don't want to take up all of your time, because I know you guys want to visit, but I've been talking with my lawyers and my accountant, and I'd like to make an offer on this house. You don't have to do any more work on it, unless you want to, of course. The normal inspections don't have to apply since I'm buying it outright, but I would like to have them so I know what I'm dealing with."

"Wow. I wasn't expecting that," Mertie said, looking a little relieved.

Olive figured that she and Garnet probably didn't make a whole lot and would appreciate the money from the sale since the money that they were supposed to be getting from their parents' business had been held up, although as far as she knew, that was working out, and it wouldn't be long, maybe another month or two, until it was straightened away.

"I would love to have you buy it. It would be great to have it go into the hands of people we know. I thought about buying it myself, but Hobert really wants to stay down by the shore, and while he would live here if I wanted him to, it seems kind of ostentatious."

Olive smiled. Amara had changed so much since becoming involved with Hobert. All changes in a good way. He'd been such a great influence on her, bringing her back from being a workaholic and hardly ever around her family to wanting to have relationships with all of her sisters.

"I'm willing to pay fair market value. I've talked to several real estate agents, and they have a figure in mind, but as long as your figure is in the ballpark, that's what I'll pay."

"Well, it's funny you should mention it, because I just got the appraisal back from our agent yesterday. It's actually here on my phone," Mertie said, picking up her phone and scrolling through until she found the email she was looking for.

She listed the amount that her agent had said.

"That's actually less than I was quoted. I'm totally fine with that amount, as long as you guys are. I don't want anyone to feel like they were cheated. And I don't want you to give me any kind of breaks just because..." He looked at Olive but didn't say anything.

Olive looked back at him, then glanced at her sisters, who smiled knowingly.

She wanted to tell them that things weren't like that, but she supposed they probably looked that way since he had basically been staying here to take care of her.

"We won't. We promise," Mertie said, breaking into Olive's train of thought.

"All right. I just wanted to throw that out there. I'm not in a huge rush, although I wouldn't mind getting it settled before fall. That will give me the winter to make any changes that I need and... I've been thinking about buying the house I'm living in."

That was news to Olive, and her brows lifted.

"We can talk about it later. I had a big phone call this morning and didn't have a chance to chat with you before your sisters came."

"That's fine. I appreciate you letting me know," she said, although not sure why that applied to her. He certainly didn't owe her anything and definitely not information on his business dealings.

But she didn't go into all of that with her siblings sitting there.

Once the door closed behind him, Mertie squeezed her hand. "That's amazing. How did you talk him into buying this house?"

"I didn't. Although I guess I did know he was thinking about it."

"She's been in bed this whole week. She's supposed to be resting so she can make it to my wedding and do more than stand on the dance floor and look like she's going to faint," Amara said, patting Olive's hand.

"You're not even going to have a dance floor," she said, remembering that the last time she had talked to Amara, they were going to get married at the church and have the dinner on the grounds, asking people to bring their own lawn chairs and a dish to share. They had a few tables they could set up to hold the food, but everybody was going to be eating from paper plates on their lap.

"Have you seen the weather for tomorrow?" Amara asked as she pulled up her phone.

"If it's supposed to be sunny, God will handle it, and if you get rain, you know who's in charge of that too," Mertie said, not in a dismissive, lecturing way, but in a tone that was most likely designed to make Amara feel better.

"I know you're right. I just need to have faith that God's going to work it out, but I really, really want a sunny day for my wedding."

"God knows that too," Mertie said.

She couldn't remember too many times where she and her sisters had sat and talked growing up, but Olive couldn't think of too many other things she'd rather do than sit and listen to them.

"So are you guys going to be living here?" Amara asked.

"Livvy and me?" she tried to clarify, not quite knowing who else she might have meant by "you guys."

"And Doyle. He's buying the house."

"No. We're not going to live together. I mean, it's a big house, I know that, but that's not right."

"After you get married," Amara said, her tone almost saying that Olive was being dense.

"We haven't talked about getting married."

"You haven't? I guess I just assumed—"

"I assumed too. That's the story that's going around town anyway."

Olive sat against the pillows, leaning her head against the wall. How could the story have started? She hadn't said anything.

Would Cassie have been spreading stories about her? Surely not.

"I'm not sure how that got started, but we haven't talked about marriage at all. We haven't really talked about much of anything."

"You didn't need to talk at my wedding. You were dancing so close."

"That's because he was afraid I was going to fall over if he let go of me. It really didn't have anything to do with how much he likes me or anything about our relationship."

"You can tell yourself that if you want to," Mertie said, lifting her brows like she knew better.

"About the house," Olive said, wanting to get the conversation off her and Doyle. She had no idea where their relationship was.

"Hasn't he been taking care of you all of this time?" Amara continued like Olive hadn't changed the subject.

"He has. He's been doing everything. All I had to do is get myself to the bathroom and take an occasional shower. He feeds the baby, he's woken with her at night and fed her then, changed her diapers, and bathed her. He's brought me food or had Cassie do it, and he's walked beside me every day when we got out to get a little air in the morning and again in the evening. I couldn't have found a better caretaker."

"Do you think a man would do that for just anyone?" Amara asked.

It was a leading question, Olive knew that, but... She wasn't quite sure how to take it.

"Well... No. But—"

"Okay, so, no, a man doesn't do that for just anyone. He does it for the woman that he cares strongly about. Maybe even loves." Amara looked down her nose at Olive, as though daring her to disagree.

"But Doyle is different. Doyle is the kind of man who helps anyone who needs it with anything that they need. He's not going to just dump me on the side of the road because I can't take care of myself."

"He's not going to move in, take care of your every need, as well as every need of your two-month-old baby, unless he has some pretty strong feelings about you. Feelings that I believe begin with the letter L."

"He hasn't said anything about it," Olive finally said, not knowing how else to respond to her sisters. They seemed to be insisting that Doyle felt something for her that he hadn't mentioned at all. And it was true that he had held her in his arms, and they had danced together, and it was also true that he had asked her why she came back, but that didn't really mean anything, did it? She didn't want to make assumptions, because she didn't want to get hurt.

"I know I'm very fond of him. Very fond."

"Fond? Is that the best you can do?" Amara said, crossing her arms over her chest like Olive was being a bratty child.

"I don't know. I'm not sure what it feels like to be in love. I had a lot of strong feelings for Ricardo, Livvy's father, but... They evaporated as soon as he left me. It wasn't like I pined for him. And he didn't really inspire me to want to be better. In fact, he convinced me to be worse than what I knew to be good."

"And that's not true love," Mertie said firmly, drawing Olive's eyes to her. "I think that love needs to be less of a feeling and more of what Doyle has been doing. Acts of sacrifice, service, showing how he feels, rather than just saying it. Acting on what's right, rather than how he feels."

"I guess we'll just have to talk about it. I know that I've never met anyone else who's treated me as good as what he has. He seems to love me...even when I can't figure out why. And he's definitely taking great care of my daughter, which probably means more to me than anything else." It was so true. She felt like she could trust Doyle with her daughter, like he truly cared about her, like he loved her like she was his own, and that was probably the thing more than anything else that pulled at her heartstrings and made her want to be the very best she could for him.

"Maybe he hasn't said anything because of you being sick. It's also been only a couple of weeks that you've been back. But I've never thought it's been a good idea to wait for a long time when you know for sure you're with the one God has for you. If you have the same values, and you're sure that you're following God's leading, dating, or the equivalent, is a bad idea. We should make a decision and follow through with it." Mertie nodded her head to emphasize her words.

"But you definitely need to make sure that it's God's will. Because it's a major, life-changing decision. And one that you can't get out of."

"Well, you can," Olive said, looking at Amara.

"You know what I mean," Amara said, and Olive had to agree. She didn't even want to think the D word, but that was the only way to undo a bad decision of that magnitude. And it had implications that stretched not just between the couple who was divorcing, but their children and their families and generations to come, because the family would be split. Hearts would be broken, and there would be pain in every corner. She didn't want to do that to anyone, not to her sisters, most especially not to Doyle.

"Guys, I don't even know why we're talking about this. Doyle hasn't said anything at all about getting married."

"I think all Amara and I are saying is that he will." Mertie looked smug, and then she completely changed the subject. "So, how do you guys feel about selling the house to Doyle?"

"I'm in. I don't care what he pays. It's not like we need the money." Amara's words were firm.

"I don't want to make a rash decision, but I agree with you. It doesn't really matter what he gives us, although it's very fair of him to give us exactly what our realtor says it's worth. And I'm totally fine with it."

They both looked at Olive. Like she had a deciding vote.

She enjoyed the moment for just a minute, because moments with her sisters had been few and far between.

"Are both of you staying in Raspberry Ridge?" she asked.

Surprise registered on both of their faces, probably because they weren't expecting her to change the subject, and they both nodded.

"I don't know where God might lead us, but for right now, we have zero plans of ever leaving the town we love. This is where we plan to put down roots and raise our family. And serve the church as long as they'll have us."

"This is where I grew up, and where my best memories are, and it's where Hobert grew up too. We have no plans of leaving. He's going to continue to fish, and we'll keep the money that we get from my parents aside, just in case regulations ever force him out of the water. Then we'll have something to fall back on. But hopefully that will mean that we can stay here. Because that's what we want."

"That's what I want too. I was hoping that I would be able to buy the house, with my equity in it and especially after hearing that we were supposed to be getting money from our parents' business, but... I can't afford it. Not now. Maybe if we held off for six months."

"You want us to?" Amara asked gently.

She shook her head. It wasn't fair for her to keep the sale of the house from going through, when they had a buyer and he was eager. She knew her sisters seemed to think that Doyle and she were inevitably going to get married, but she didn't have that impression, and he hadn't said a word. But she supposed there wasn't anyone she would rather buy the house, and she also was sure that he would be fine if she lived in it until she could get back on her feet. Or at least until the payments from her parents' business started coming in.

"Yes. I want Doyle to buy it if that's possible. I'm all in."

The conversation turned to Amara's wedding and the plans that she and Hobert had for their house on the beach. It was simple, beautifully so, and there was going to be so much love in the house that Olive figured it didn't really matter what it looked like, although it was going to be beautiful.

Amara had that way of being able to take what she touched and turn it into beauty.

"We'll see you tomorrow morning, okay?" Amara said after two hours had gone by and they were ready to leave.

"I'm feeling really good. And I'm really looking forward to it. If there's anything that I can do to help, you'll be sure to ask?"

"If we have any last-minute things that need to be done, I've got you on speed dial," Amara said, holding up her phone before shoving it in her pocket and walking out the door in front of Mertie who blew a kiss at her as she left.

Twenty-Five

"What do you think? Is it pretty?" Doyle sat in front of Livvy who was propped in a bouncer seat, outside on the patio that overlooked the lake. Neither one of them were looking at the lake though. He held a shiny diamond ring up in front of Livvy, and the baby gurgled and cooed, and her little hand swiped at it.

"No. It's not for you. It's for Mommy. Do you think I should try to give it to her today?"

It was fast, a lot faster than he would ever have moved with anyone else, but no one had ever been like Olive to him. He hadn't quite felt like they'd picked up where they'd left off back before she'd gone away, but he did feel like they had a connection that he never felt with anyone else. He also admired her in a way he'd never admired anyone.

"You like it?" he said to Livvy who just looked happy to be there.

"I'm afraid she's going to tell me no. Or maybe she's going to tell me that I'm going too fast. Or I couldn't possibly feel for her what I do. But it's deeper than that, you know?" He was talking to a baby, and he knew it. But she enjoyed listening to him, and he didn't mind getting his words out in the open. He had thought about talking to Pastor Garnet, but with his own wedding, and then the wedding of his sister-in-law coming up and all the other things that had been going on in their lives, he hadn't wanted to add to the drama.

Plus, as a man, he felt like he should be able to figure this out on his own. It was almost like stopping to ask for directions. He was one of those guys who would rather drive around for an extra three hours than stop and ask. He thought the figuring-it-out part was fun.

This was less fun than nerve-wracking.

"So when you talk to Mommy later, you put in a good word for me, okay?" he said to the baby.

She gave him one of her adorable, toothless smiles and grabbed for the ring, which was beautiful as the sunlight shimmered off it.

He'd bought it almost a decade ago, when he thought they were going to get married the first time. And kept it all that time. For some reason, he brought it with him when he moved to Raspberry Ridge. There were a lot of things he left behind, but this ring wasn't one of them.

"This represents a pretty big commitment. It's not something that should be entered into lightly. But I don't think that a couple is supposed to hem and haw around, waiting for years, trying to figure out whether they're with the right person or not. If they are, they should get married, and if they're just messing around, they should stop, because that's not right." Those were just his opinions, although he felt like he could back them up with principles from the Bible.

Regardless, his opinions might not be Olive's opinions, and that was one thing about getting married. You had to take into account the other person for the rest of your life. It wasn't something that he had considered when he was a young kid. Thinking about someone else all the time. Now, he found, over the last week anyway, that he actually enjoyed working to make her happy. Giving up what he wanted, for her. Sure, there were hard times, especially in the middle of the night when he really didn't want to get up, but... For the most part, serving her fulfilled him in a way that he hadn't anticipated.

"I'm not sure I have enough nerve. I really don't know how she feels. I suppose I ought to try to figure that out before I drop her ring on her unexpectedly," he said, giving the ring one more tilt in the sun before putting it back in its blue velvet box and snapping the lid closed. He dropped the box in his pocket and looked back at the baby.

"I just want to say, you're not much help."

She grinned at him, grabbing a hold of his finger and sticking it in her mouth, gumming on it.

"Are you hungry? Or are you just doing that because it's some weird instinct that babies have?"

He'd done some research on babies online, since he'd never actually been around any in real life and certainly hadn't had any instruction in them. He wanted to do a good job. Taking care of Olive's little one.

"Da da da da," Livvy said. He figured she wasn't saying it to him; it was just a noise that babies had a tendency to make, according to what he read online, but he couldn't stop the little thrill that went straight to his heart.

"I want that. Want to be your daddy. We're going to have to figure out a way to talk Mom into it. Actually, I don't want to talk her into it. I want her to want it too. But one human can't really make another human want to do something that they don't want to do. That's one of the lessons that you'll eventually learn in life. Hopefully anyway. It took me a little while to figure that out. Maybe when I was watching your mom leave me and knew that I was powerless to stop her. It was painful."

He didn't really want to talk about bad things with Livvy, so his voice trailed off as he thought about how badly he had wanted to hold onto her and never let her go, but he had known that with love, a person wanted the best for the other person, and sometimes that meant prying up their fingers and allowing them to leave.

"The hardest thing I've ever done," he said seriously to Livvy who studied him with her big, dark eyes.

Sometimes the eyes reminded him that her father was a world away, with another family, and while it made him feel a little bit jealous, the fact that Olive obviously thought a lot of him to have been with him to the point where she had a child with him, it also made him feel bad for Livvy, the fact that she most likely would never know him. And he was okay with that. He had no idea what he was missing. Livvy was a sweetheart with her own developing personality. Very laid-back.

Easygoing and inquisitive. He couldn't imagine getting tired of watching her.

"I don't think I'm nearly as interesting,"

"I'm not sure what you're comparing yourself to, but you are a very interesting man."

He jerked his head around, watching as Olive finished walking out the door, two glasses of water in her hands.

"How'd you know I was thirsty?" he said, standing up to meet her. Wanting to tell her that she shouldn't have come down without checking with him, but she had done everything he had asked her to do, including staying in bed and only texting him when she wanted to get up. Today was the first day that she got up on her own. He couldn't complain.

"I just had a hunch. Or maybe it was a peace offering."

That made him smile. "You thought if you brought me a glass of water, I wouldn't notice that you are out of bed and had come down the stairs without telling me?"

"Something like that," she said as she bent down in front of Livvy, smiling in her face and kissing her forehead as Livvy reached for her cheeks and her nose. "I think she's grown and changed just in the six days I've been sick. She looks so big. Like a little baby instead of a newborn."

"She has been growing and changing fast." He almost told her that Livvy had said "da da" just a few minutes ago, but decided not to, knowing that it was just a noise, and not really the baby calling him her daddy, plus, not wanting to throw that out there and make Olive any more uncomfortable than what she already had to be around him. After all, he was almost her jailer.

"I was kind of hoping we could take a walk. I mean usually we do in the evening, and it's almost evening."

It was about four o'clock in the afternoon, so maybe an hour or so before they usually did it. Usually he waited until the end of the day when he was sure he wouldn't be getting any more business calls.

"We can put her in a stroller and head to the healing garden. How does that sound?"

"Oh? I'm going to be allowed to walk on more than just the driveway today?"

"If you think you can make it."

"I think I can. I just had a good visit with my sisters, then a nice nap, and now I have a handsome man and a beautiful baby to go walking with me. What more could a girl want?"

He almost said a husband, but he honestly didn't know whether she thought that would be a good thing or not.

He was going to be buying the house right out from underneath her, and he didn't know whether she would have a place to stay or not. He didn't want to hold that over her head, like he had told Mertie.

They didn't say much as he moved away from the bouncer seat to the stroller, checking to make sure her diaper was still dry since he had just changed it less than thirty minutes prior when she had finished her bottle.

Olive seemed like she almost had a spring in her step, and he had to admit that she did seem a good bit better.

"I feel so much better, my arms don't feel like they weigh a ton, and dragging myself out of bed doesn't feel like a day's worth of work." She lifted her face to the sunshine as though enjoying its brightness shining down on her. "I owe you a lot. I owe you thanks, and gratitude for everything you've done for me."

"You don't owe me anything. I did it because I wanted to. And... I guess I wanted you to know that I'm...fond of you."

Fond. That wasn't the word he meant. He wanted to say more.

"Fond?" She lifted her brows and then laughed. "I think I just used that word when I was telling my sisters how I felt about you. And they laughed at me."

"They did?"

"They insisted that I felt more than fondness toward you."

"Do you?" He couldn't keep the hope that leapt into his chest down. He wanted her to feel more, for them to be going on this emotional journey together. Not just him by himself.

"I guess I feel like feelings aren't what I should be basing any relationship on. I've done that once, and it bit me hard."

"I see." He tried not to allow his disappointment to show on his face. "What are you going to be basing your next relationship on?"

"I want someone who is steadfast, has integrity and character," she said thoughtfully, looking down at the pavement as they slowly walked down the drive. "I want someone I can depend on. Someone who's going to be there for me when I need it." She sighed. "Ricardo couldn't get away from me fast enough when I got sick, and he definitely wasn't there when I had Livvy. As soon as things got a little bit hard, he dropped me."

He wanted to point out that he hadn't dropped her. That things had gotten hard, and he'd stepped up. But he hadn't done that to earn brownie points. He'd done it because...he wanted to.

"You didn't do that. I want a man like you." She looked up, meeting his eyes as he glanced down at her. He knew his mouth was hanging open, but he didn't know how to get it closed and wipe the surprise off his face.

She laughed. "I can see I surprised you. I'm not saying that I'm going to force you to marry me, and I understand our history. It's not the best, and it's my fault. I can apologize, but I can't erase it. I can't make you think any better of me—"

"You don't have to try to make me think better of you. I already think the world of you."

She tilted her head and glanced at him. He tightened his hands on the stroller. He didn't want to mess this up. He wanted to say all the right words, but there just wasn't anything in his head. Especially after she had said that she wanted a man just like him. He wanted to take that as a compliment, but part of him said, instead of saying a man just like him, she should have said him. Just him.

"Still, I can't take that away. And I don't expect you to forget."

"I don't think that's something I could forget, but I do think it's something that we could work past." He said those words cautiously, because he wasn't quite sure what she was saying. Did she want him? Or didn't she? And then he figured it probably shouldn't matter. He could just tell her how he felt, and then she could say whether she wanted him or not. The thing was, if she didn't want him, it was going to be awkward while they redefined their relationship after he admitted that he still loved her just as much, if not more than he used to.

"Do you think we could?" she asked, and there was definitely hope in her voice.

"I would like to. I...just asked Livvy for permission to marry you. I'm not sure that she said yes, but she seemed pretty happy about it. You've noticed she's smiling, right?"

"Yes, isn't she cute? Wait. What? You...asked Livvy, my daughter, if you could marry me?" Her steps slowed as she put her fingers on his forearm. He slowed with her. "As in...you'd marry me?"

"As in, I have a ring, and I showed it to her. I think she liked it. I asked her if she thought I could give it to her mommy, and then I thought maybe it was too soon. Maybe I would be pushing you. Maybe you didn't feel the same about me as I feel about you. I thought that maybe I should ask."

They'd made it down to the bottom of the drive, but instead of turning on the sidewalk to walk up to the healing garden, they stopped and faced each other.

"You're kidding, right?" she said faintly.

"Why? Is it that scary to think about marrying me?" He knew that that was the problem last time, it scared her. She was afraid to commit. She ran away instead. "Am I going to make you run away again? I've been worried about that."

"No. I'm not running. I decided that that part of my life is over. No more running. I stand and face things, no matter how much I would like to leave. I need to work things out with people, rather than walking away from them. I think that's more biblical."

"I definitely agree with you. I don't see any instances where Jesus walked away from people. He went through the hard parts of the relationship, and he just kept forgiving and loving and serving and... That's what I want to do."

"I don't want to make you have to do that. A relationship with me shouldn't be all about walking through the fire all the time." She looked a little annoyed. It made him smile.

"I think there are going to be plenty of good times. If you're saying what I think you're saying."

She paused, looking up at him, and then whispered, "That I love you?"

He closed his eyes. He'd waited for years to hear her say that. Literally years. He couldn't believe that she just had, and he wanted to hear the words again

"Now you're the one who's scared?" she asked, a little bit of fear creeping into her voice.

"No. I'm the one who wants to hear them again."

"I love you." She smiled as he opened his eyes and saw her lips spread upward.

He put his hand in his pocket, pulled out the box, and knelt down on one knee.

Opening the lid, he said, "This is the ring Livvy approved of. I bought it back when we were together before and had been planning to ask you to marry me...sometime. I wasn't sure when. But I carried it around with me a few times and had it in my pocket the day you told me you were leaving. I don't think that means it's bad luck, I just wanted you to know that I hadn't bought it for someone else. It was yours all these years."

She lifted a finger and touched the edge of the box. "It's beautiful. I can't believe you had it that long. That you bought it when you were, what, nineteen?"

"Yeah. It was pretty expensive, and I was tempted to sell it to finance my internship, but I just couldn't let go. Would you do me the honor of becoming my wife?"

Twenty-Six

Olive stared at the ring. Then she looked at the man holding it. She couldn't believe how God had smiled at her. Especially after she messed everything up. She didn't deserve a man like this.

"Yes. I will. I'll spend the rest of my life trying to make sure you don't regret this day." She made that promise and knew she could keep it. She wasn't the spoiled brat she had been all those years ago when he had almost asked for the first time. She had lived a lot, and suffered a little, and knew what a gift God had just dropped in her lap. A man like Doyle didn't come around every day, and she would cherish him for the amazing miracle he was.

He pushed to his feet and pulled the ring out of the box. "Would you like to wear it?"

"I would. Do you think it'll fit?" she asked as he was pushing it over her finger.

"You told me your ring size way back then, I forget why. Something about a birthstone or a class ring or something, and it was a number that stuck in my head. So, it might not now, but I did get the number from you."

"I can't believe I don't even remember any conversation that we ever had about a ring."

"It was very much in passing. But I guess that's what I was always looking toward. I didn't really believe in dating just for the sake of wasting time with someone. I always felt like you should be building toward something, or you shouldn't be doing it at all."

"Those are wise words. I wish I had lived by those. But I guess there's always going to be regrets, although I can't really imagine my life turning out any better than it is right now."

"Me either. I..." He looked around.

They were in the middle of town. So, it surprised her when he said, "Is it okay if I kiss you?"

She felt a thrill to the very depths of her soul, and she couldn't stop her lips from turning up into the biggest possible smile so that her face felt like it was stretched in two because her smile was so big.

"I would really love that."

His eyes crinkled at the corners as his hand came up and cupped her cheek. "I hope I haven't coerced you into this in any way. I feel a little bit like I'm taking advantage of someone who was sick."

"My body was sick, my brain is just fine. I wanted this but didn't know how to get it. I wasn't sure how you felt. My sisters hinted at it, but I didn't believe them."

"Maybe they knew better than I did. Although, I did have the ring. So maybe I suspected this might happen. Regardless, I love you. I always will."

His words wrapped around her heart and squeezed as his head lowered toward hers, and they sealed the promises they just made with the sweetest kiss she'd ever had in her entire life. She couldn't blame her dizziness on her illness, but it didn't matter, because he was right there for her to hold onto, as his arms wrapped around her, and she clung to him.

"I waited a lot of years for that," he said roughly as he lifted his head. "And it was better than anything I had imagined. This is better. You and me. I can hardly believe it's true."

"It's true," she said seriously, and then she grinned. "I wonder what Pastor Garnet would say if we ask him to marry us next Friday?"

That made Doyle laugh out loud. "He might think we're just a little bit crazy, but maybe he's expecting it too, because you said your sisters were hinting, and one of those sisters is married to him."

"That's a good point. I don't think we'll surprise him at all, although, as busy as his schedule was, we probably ought to tell him right away so that he can pencil us in. It seemed like he was in pretty high demand."

"Raspberry Ridge has been without a pastor for a while, and before that, Pastor Calvin had been slowing down. I'm sure he's going to be in high demand for a while. But I agree. We better put our names on his schedule."

They grinned at each other, amused at their little shared joke. It wasn't terribly funny, but it was fun to share humor with someone she loved. It made her feel closer to him, like the two of them had a little world all their own.

"As much as I would like to stand here and kiss you, I think we ought to finish our walk. It's good for you, and I probably need it too," Doyle said, giving her a little wink.

She laughed at his wink and took his arm as he took a hold of the stroller and they started back up the walk.

When they reached the healing garden, they could see that someone was already in it.

"Do we want to disturb her?" Olive asked softly, nodding at the girl who walked with her hands clasped behind her, staring at the water.

"I don't think we'll disturb her if we go on in and sit down at the bench, and she almost looks like she wants someone to talk to," he said.

She realized he was right. She did look a little lost, a little sad, and maybe she needed someone to cheer her up or a stranger to give her a listening ear.

"It won't be very private if we're chatting with a stranger," she said, looking up at him, hoping that that wasn't going to change his mind about wanting to sit with her. Ricardo didn't seem to want to have too much to do with her if they couldn't be alone. It was like her company wasn't any fun. It was just kissing her and other things that he really wanted.

Looking back, she wished she had been smarter and had seen that right away. Or had paid attention to the nagging thoughts that gripped her when she was around him.

"That's okay with me. Just having you with me is enough. I can't think of anything that having you won't make better."

She gave him a smile, probably one of those sappy, love-filled smiles that people who were in love gave to each other all the time. She never thought that she would be one of those people, and yet here she was.

He opened the gate, and she walked through holding it while he pushed the stroller through. Livvy had fallen asleep on their walk.

It would be a fun story to tell her that they had gotten engaged while she slept in the stroller beside them. She could hardly wait for Livvy to grow up and to be of an age where she could tell her stories like that. But she didn't want to wish the baby years away. They were so short and fleeting.

"I hope we're not bothering you," she said to the young girl as she turned around as they approached.

"Not at all. This isn't my personal place, as much time as I spend here."

"I've been ill, so I guess I haven't noticed that you've been around," she said.

"I'm Becky," the girl said, holding out her hand. "I just moved to Raspberry Ridge, and I'm renting the old rundown farm that's back by the Brandstetters."

"It's nice to meet you, Becky. I'm Olive, and I grew up here. But then I moved away for a while. And this is my...fiancé, Doyle. He grew up here too. We're both back to stay."

It felt so good to say that. To introduce Doyle as her fiancé, and to say that they were back to stay. This was where she was going to put down roots. This is the home that she had always sought. This was where she and Doyle would raise their family.

She smiled a little at that thought. She didn't even know if he wanted to have more children. She did, but she could understand that he might not. Kids were a lot of work. She knew that now. And she hadn't even been the one to take care of Livvy for most of her life so far. She'd been too sick herself.

Becky shook her hand and then shook Doyle's hand.

"If you don't mind, I see Homer over there, and I wanted to have a word with him. Can I leave you two here?"

Doyle looked her in the eyes, and it was like there was a silent message going between them. She remembered the words he had said earlier, thinking that the young girl looked like she had some problems and maybe could use a listening ear. She thought that might be what he was doing now, leaving so Becky might feel free to talk, where she might not feel as easy with a man standing near.

"Sure. Maybe if Becky wants, we can chat for a bit. I'm not familiar with the farm she's talking about, and I'm curious."

Doyle squeezed her shoulder and then said, "If you don't mind, I'll just go ahead and push Livvy. I think she'll stay asleep if the stroller stays moving."

"That's just fine."

They strolled off, and Olive looked back at Becky.

"Is that your daughter?"

"Mine, not his." She didn't want Becky to think that Doyle was that kind of man. Which was the logical assumption. Although, she thought that Doyle might take umbrage at the fact that she made a distinction with Livvy. He might want to be included when she talked about her parents. Regardless, once they were married, it wouldn't matter. But for now, the only one in the relationship who had loose morals was her.

"I see. He seems to adore her."

"He does. I... Sometimes God gives you something that you don't deserve. That's what happened when God gave me Doyle."

Becky smiled as though she thought that was sweet.

"I just had malaria not that long ago, and I'm still recovering. Would you like to go sit down for a little bit? I really would like to hear about your farm."

"Sure," Becky said, turning with Olive and walking down the path. "I'd like to buy it, but it's a little bit more money than what I can afford."

"What are you planning on doing with that?" she asked. She'd wanted to ask whether a single woman would be able to handle a farm by herself, but she didn't want to insult Becky.

"I grew up near Strawberry Sands. I...have adopted parents there now. But I feel like I am taking advantage of them and keeping them from doing everything that they could with their natural children, so I thought I ought to move out."

"How do your parents feel about that?" Olive asked, knowing that she hoped that Doyle would consider Livvy his, and in that case, she assumed he would be very hurt if she left thinking that she was leaving more room for his "real" children.

"They say that they're sad. They want me to come back, but sometimes you just need to get away, you know?"

Boy, could Olive ever tell her about that.

"I felt like that at one time."

"Did you?" Becky asked as they came to the bench and settled down beside the soft waterfall. Flowers bloomed in profusion around them, and with the blue sky and the lake breeze, it felt like a perfect place. Calm and restful.

"I did," she said, trying to think of what she could say.

"And how did that work out?" Becky asked, seeming genuinely curious.

"Well, I hurt someone who is close to me. Quite badly actually. And it's a regret I'll carry with me throughout my life. When you hurt other people, you don't forget about that. Especially people that you love." She paused for a moment, fingering the end of her shirt and then brushing her hands down her lap. "You don't want to hurt the people who are closest to you. Sometimes you think you're making the best decisions that you can, the best decisions for yourself, sometimes even the best decisions for everyone involved, but it causes pain. I know we can learn and grow from the times that we're hurt, but you won't forget the pain you cause to the people who love you."

"So you want me to think carefully about the steps I take because you think that hurting people lasts a lifetime?"

"I definitely think you should think carefully about the steps you're taking. I know if I could go back and do things over again, I would make decisions based on what's best for others, rather than being selfish and thinking about myself. However, you always have to do what God wants you to do, no matter how that affects the people around you. It's two different things."

"I see. So doing it because it's God's will is one thing, doing it because I want to is something completely different."

"And I think you already knew that."

"I did. But sometimes what you want to do is so compelling, and sometimes the need to get away…takes precedence over everything else."

"Have you talked to your adoptive parents about your need to heal?"

"I don't want to burden them with it."

"Isn't that what parents are for?"

"I'm used to handling things on my own."

"Would you like it if someone close to you said that rather than asked you to help them?"

Becky sat there for a minute, as though thinking about what she said. "I have a little sister. I would be really hurt if she thought she could handle something really huge on her own and was afraid that drawing me into it would hurt me."

"That's probably how your adoptive parents feel about you. Unless you think that they don't love you?"

"I know they love me. There was never any doubt about that," Becky said. She fiddled with her hands in her lap for a little bit, rolling a blade of grass that she'd plucked from somewhere between her fingers before throwing it into the water. "There was a boy that I liked."

Of course. It was a lost love story. Olive almost smiled.

"And?"

"And he went away to college. He had me taking care of his horses. I did happily, until…something happened. It hurt. And… I, well, basically I came here."

"Do your parents know about this boy? Do they approve of him?"

"I think so. We were never really together together. He wanted to go to college first, and I understood that. He was a lot older than I was."

"Is he with someone else now?"

She hoped not. She hoped that Becky would say that he just had other interests. Becky seemed like such a sweet girl, and she hated to think that her heart had been broken because some guy had decided that he wanted someone else.

"I don't know. I don't know anything about him. He...stopped talking to me."

It sounded almost exactly like what Olive had done to Doyle.

"I had that happen to me. Only... I was the one who quit talking to the person who loved me and had been kinder to me than anyone else in my life before."

"That's Rodney. That's how I would describe him. The person who understood me and was kind to me when no one else was. He saw something in me that I didn't even see in myself."

"Yeah. And I ended up hurting him. And leaving him for a while."

"Did you find someone else? Is that your fiancé?"

"Actually, no. He waited for me. I don't even know if he deliberately thought about waiting for me, or if he just couldn't find anyone else. I haven't asked," she said, laughing a little and realizing that probably was a question she should have asked. "Anyway, I don't know what to say to you, other than I really appreciated the fact that when he saw me, even though I had hurt him, he always saw good in me. That probably is the reason we're together today. Because when I came back, he didn't hit me with a bunch of vitriol, even though I deserved it for what I did to him; he forgave me immediately and saw me for the best that I was, rather than the worst of what I had done."

"That's hard."

"Yeah. And a lot of years passed between the time I left and the time I came back. Time does heal."

"And distance. Maybe I should tell my parents that. I just need some distance, to try to make it so that if I ever meet him again, I can be kind."

"What were you planning on doing with your farm?" Olive asked, wondering if that might lead into her gently suggesting that Becky might be better off back with her parents.

"I wanted to do a riding stable, kind of like we did down in Strawberry Sands. I am good with horses, although I don't have a lot of money. But lots of people start out at the bottom and work their way up, and I'm not afraid to work." She looked very determined.

"Well, just know that I'm here if you want some help, although I don't have any money either, so I can't give you that kind of help."

"I don't think I would ask for it. What I can't do on my own, I can't expect someone else to invest in someone that they don't know."

"I suppose, although, sometimes there are people looking for things to invest in. And there are some people who would like to see Raspberry Ridge grow and businesses come in, including tourists, and a stable just might do the trick there."

"I'm hoping. But it's going to be slow." Becky stood slowly. "I think I'm going to go make a telephone call to my adoptive parents. Thanks for chatting with me."

"My pleasure." Olive sat looking at the waterfall for a bit, wondering if Doyle really had gone to talk to Homer and also thinking about the marriages of her sisters, and her. If she had ever thought about them getting married, she certainly would never have considered that they might get married within three weeks of each other. That was just crazy.

She had just decided to get up when her phone rang. She didn't recognize the number but swiped anyway.

"Hello?"

"Olive! I bet you don't know who this is."

"Your voice sounds familiar, but...no. I can't place it."

"Five years ago, on the Suez Canal. We shared a state room, because both of us ended up displaced, and that was the only thing available."

"Birdie! Oh my goodness. That was the best boat ride ever. And the Suez Canal, wow. Desert on both sides, water in the middle. Nothing like it."

"I know, right? And I had good company for that whole trip."

"I had the best company too."

They had begun the ride as strangers and gotten off the boat best of friends. It was not until later that she found out that Birdie was actually a world-famous pop singer. Birdie had never even mentioned it while they were on the boat. Although, she had insisted on paying for everything, because when Olive had confided to her that she was broke, expecting Birdie to say the same thing, Birdie had said not to worry about it, the trip was on her. And she had been true to her word.

That wasn't why Olive loved her, but her generous heart was definitely a part of her personality that was beautiful inside and out.

"So what's going on? Why are you calling?"

"I was just hoping your phone number had stayed the same. Unlike me. I've changed mine at least three times, because stalkers keep getting it."

"I'm sorry about that." Those were the least of her problems. She probably would never have to deal with a stalker.

"Anyway, this last tour has ruined me. I am physically and mentally exhausted in every way possible. And I remember how you talked about Raspberry Ridge and how beautiful and peaceful it was there. The serenity of being by the beach and the companionship and support of a small town. I don't know why, but I just long to be there, even though I've never seen it."

"It's a beautiful place."

"Well, I'm going to be coming. I rented a beach cottage for the summer. Starting July. I have a big tour starting in January, and I have to start practicing for it in December. But I need some quiet months to try to get my sanity back."

"Raspberry Ridge is the best place to do that."

"I figured you'd say that. But I need to do this on the down-low. I figured you'd probably figured out who I was by now, and I knew that you would recognize me. Just... I'm a regular person, okay?"

"You've never been anything but a regular person to me, special because you're my friend. Not because of anything else."

"Good to hear. I appreciate it." She took a breath and then blew it out. "All right. I have a few more shows I have to get through, and then I can crash. I can't tell you how much I'm looking forward to it."

"I wish I could help you, but I can't carry a tune in a bucket, so you're on your own, but I'm here if you need me." She paused for a second and then said, "Remember that boy I told you about?"

"The one whose heart you broke and you were wrapped up in guilt and felt bad, but said you could never go home because you couldn't face him?"

"That boy. Yes."

"What about him?"

"I'm getting married to him next Friday."

"Shut the front door," Birdie exclaimed.

"I'm dead serious. God has a really amazing way of working things out."

"I've yet to see Him work that out for me."

Olive considered pointing out to Birdie that she was a world-famous pop star, and God probably had a lot to do with that, but she refrained. Birdie was coming here for a while; they would most likely see each other and chat then. Maybe the topic would come up, or maybe it wouldn't, but whatever God allowed, she'd try to point her to Him.

"Thanks for answering. I know I probably came up unknown."

"Sure thing. I am thrilled to hear from you, and I'm really excited that you're coming to Raspberry Ridge. Even if you need to sleep and take it easy the entire time, I know you're going to love it here, and I'm excited for you."

"And I'm excited for your marriage. Congratulations. I am really glad things worked out for you."

They hung up, after promising to meet up when Birdie made it to Raspberry Ridge and had a chance to rest.

A marriage, finally recovering from her illness, and now a friend coming to visit, as well as a brand-new and very satisfying relationship with her sisters who were all planning to live in the same small town with her. She didn't think her life could get any better. It was amazing how God had worked everything out.

Twenty-Seven

"I'm not sure whether I liked Mertie's wedding better, or Amara's." Doyle spoke as he held Olive tight against him, slow dancing to whatever music was playing. Come to think of it, they were probably going a little bit slower than the music dictated, but he didn't care. He just wanted to hold her forever.

"I think they're tied in my opinion as well. And it makes me a little bit nervous, because my wedding might not measure up."

"It's not a competition." He smiled down at her. "And I can guarantee you that you're going to have the groom who's the most in love. If that means anything."

"I think that's probably one of the most important things. I have an upright, honorable man, and I don't really care what my wedding looks like."

"All right then. I wouldn't give it another thought. But I am having a good time, and the food was just as good here too."

"You think people are going to get tired of making food? Should we really ask everyone to bring another dish for another wedding?"

"I was kinda thinking that we might ask Cassie if she wanted to cater it?" He left that question open-ended, because, while he was pretty sure that Olive didn't harbor any hard feelings toward Cassie and wasn't the slightest bit concerned about any kind of feelings that he might have toward her, he didn't want to take that for granted.

"That's an awesome idea. I don't know why I didn't think of that. She could use the money, and the people in Raspberry Ridge could use a break from having to make a casserole every Friday and come to a wedding. At least they can ditch the casserole, but there's definitely going to be a wedding."

"What do you think about having it down on the pebble beach?" he asked.

"Wow. You have really great ideas. Are you sure you haven't planned a wedding before?"

"Maybe I've spent a lot of time thinking about yours and my wedding, but it's the first, and hopefully only, wedding I'll ever plan."

"I don't know, maybe you have a future as a wedding planner, because I think that's a really great idea. I wonder if that'll be enough time for Cassie?"

"And she'd probably want some kind of idea of the number of people coming, and then we're getting into a little bit more figuring than what I want to. You think there's about the same number of people here as was at Mertie's wedding?"

"I think so. You're saying you think we can probably figure on the same number coming to ours?" She tilted her head and leaned back just a little.

"Bingo."

"I agree with that." Olive moved her head and laid it on his chest.

He looked out at the people who had come to celebrate Amara and Hobert's nuptials. Funny that they had been brought up to dislike Hobert without even knowing why and that Amara ended up marrying him.

"I think Dabney has found her purpose in life," Doyle said.

"Dabney?" She lifted her head and looked around, smiling when she finally found her. "Oh my goodness. She's with Dominic and Vera, a twin in each arm, and two kids grabbing onto her dress, begging her to go play with them."

"And the other two kids are at the door, motioning for her to come. I think she has an entourage."

"I think Vera and Dominic can use a little break. And Dabney is so responsible. She's probably the one teenager in the entire world who can handle six kids better than most adults."

"I can't argue with that." He looked down at the baby sleeping in the car seat. "I have a feeling that Livvy is going to be just as good with children as what Dabney is."

"What gives you that idea?"

"Well, I guess I should talk to you about it, but I was thinking we would have at least six of our own, maybe more."

"Really? After all the work that a baby is, you want six or more?"

"Well, doesn't the Bible say that we're supposed to populate the world?"

"Don't you think that's already been done?" she asked, with not a little bit of irony in her voice. "Eight billion people is pretty populated."

"But the birth rate of Americans is going down. We can do what we can to combat that and keep our country populated. Plus, God actually said to be fruitful and multiply. That probably means we should have at least three. But that really isn't multiplication, when two become three. It should be four or six or something like that."

"You're really set on that number six."

"I'm happy with ten. We can compromise."

"Hmm. I think I'm going to have to think about that for a little bit."

"Yeah. Maybe eight. That's a nice middle-of-the-road number."

"I think you're teasing me," she said, looking up into his eyes with a glint in her own. "But I like the idea of having a bunch of little redheaded kids, tall and lanky with your teasing green eyes."

"You like my eyes, huh?"

"I like all of you," she corrected.

He smiled, and she laid her head on his chest again.

He knew there would be hard times ahead, no life was without them, but he had a godly woman by his side, and he had a God who was in control of everything. They would face the golden dawn together. It was all a man could ask for.

Epilogue

Birdie Pollock stood at the door of the cottage that she'd just bought, sight unseen.

When the advertisement had said rustic, she had thought country chic, not dilapidated, rundown, barely inhabitable.

Well, her bad.

She blew out a breath, thinking about what she could do. She had plenty of money. It wasn't like she was stuck here. But she'd gone out of her way to lay tracks that pointed to different destinations, that would hopefully keep the paparazzi off her trail, and so far, it had worked. No one seemed to know she was here. She'd been dead quiet on social media, and she hadn't seen a single vehicle that looked like it contained a reporter for the last hundred miles.

She'd cut her hair, dyed it, donned glasses, and wore clothes that did not say pop star. The ragged jeans, ill-fitting T-shirt, and purse that she picked up at the dollar store were not anything that the paparazzi would expect to photograph her in.

Regardless, she had avoided the celebration that had been going on down at the beach. She'd heard it when she stopped to look at the healing garden. Olive had told her all about it and sung its virtues, and she couldn't help but hear the music and celebration that was going on below.

It must be Olive's wedding. And she was happy for her friend but a little bit sad for herself. She had five serious relationships in the last ten years, and all of them had ended up being about money. Three of the five guys had been paid more than one million dollars to go away quietly into the night. Two of the guys had sold their stories to tabloids, and the internet had been abuzz for months afterward.

She knew that that just came with the life of a world-famous pop singer, but she didn't have to like it.

And she could learn from them. No man for her. None. She was done with relationships until she was done with her career, because the only thing that men seemed to want out of her was money and fame. Not necessarily in that order. Two of the guys that she dated had gone on to sign huge television contracts, one for a reality TV show and one to be a judge on some star-seeking show.

She stood on the stoop, walking over the porch, afraid to go in. There was another cabin, just fifty feet away, and she realized that she probably should have bought it too.

She hadn't known it existed though, none of the pictures that she'd seen had shown it.

She'd no sooner thought that than a car pulled up. It was a 1970s version, or somewhere thereabouts. She was hardly an expert on cars, but it was old and dilapidated, almost as old and dilapidated as the cabin that it pulled up to.

That was fine. Hopefully that was a local resident, and they didn't have internet or TV and wouldn't have the slightest idea of who she was.

She crossed her fingers, hoping for an old man or young girl to get out of the car, but as had been her luck lately, someone her own age unwound his lanky frame from the car.

Great, a man. Just the type of thing she did not want to see.

She almost laughed. After all, the world was half men. Still, she was here to get away from them, and everything else, and to rest and recover.

Which made her turn back to the cabin and look inside once more.

The beds were filthy, the stove covered in cobwebs, and she was pretty sure that the shower didn't have a door on it. Or a curtain or anything. She was used to tile showers that were spotlessly clean, this was...disgusting.

How was she supposed to get any rest in here?

But she didn't have much of a choice, and she was exhausted after driving for several hours from the Chicago airport.

Deciding that the floor was cleaner than the bed, she shook out the blanket she held, laid it out on the floor, dropped her pillow on top of it, and lay down. There would be time enough to try to figure out what to do, but she was going to take a nap first. Too late, she thought about locking her door. Maybe the man beside her was a serial killer.

At this point in her life, she was too exhausted to get up and fix the problem. If he wanted to kill her, he could have at it.

Join Jessie's list and be the first to know about new releases and sales on her books!

Read Beyond the Setting Sun, the next book in the Raspberry Ridge series where a world-famous pop singer and a super star hockey player rent neighboring cabins on the beach. Will their grandparents play matchmakers? Secret identity, forced proximity and cute kids fill this story to the brim! Keep reading for a sneak peek now.

Sneak peek of Beyond the Setting Sun

Wesley Moffat, hockey superstar and potential author, if his agent had anything to do with it, sat on the front porch of the lake house he'd bought not long ago. Staring at the water, and contemplating his future.

His agent had insisted that if he had any hope of repairing his reputation in the professional hockey league, he would need to get his autobiography finished by the time his suspension was over and he was allowed to join his teammates on the Virginia Icebreakers.

He couldn't imagine a life without hockey, although he'd come close to losing everything. He needed to get this book done.

The publishing world worked slower than a tortoise, and the book wouldn't come out until next summer, but hopefully by then, he would have helped his team win the championship cup, and the book would just be the icing on top. If anything else went wrong, it might help fans understand why he was the way he was, according to his agent, and perhaps save his reputation and career.

Wesley didn't give a flip about his reputation, but his career was important to him.

And he was back to where he started. He couldn't imagine his life without hockey.

He sat and stared at the computer in front of him. Lots of folks he knew had ghostwriters, and Wesley could get on board with it. The only problem with a ghostwriter was details of his memoir might be leaked, and that would ruin everything according to his agent, Jim.

Jim was good at what he did, but sometimes he could be a little bit paranoid, at least in Wesley's opinion.

"It's a little burnt, but it's edible." His grandfather lived with him so when Wesley went to the beach for the summer, he came with, came out of the screen door of the cabin—no air conditioning—and handed him a plate of...maybe chicken?

Neither one of them could cook worth anything, and they were close to being in danger of starving. There were no fast-food restaurants in Raspberry Ridge.

He'd picked the town out, not because of its beautiful views of the lake, but because of its seclusion and isolation. There shouldn't be any paparazzi or anyone who would actually recognize him. Especially if he kept a low profile.

The downside was, when one of them burnt supper, there were no fast-food restaurants within thirty minutes.

Tonight, it was Gramps's turn to burn supper. Last night, it had been him. Fish. Fish wasn't his favorite anyway, and it almost tasted better burnt. Gramps didn't think so, but people could have other opinions from him. They could be wrong.

"Thanks. This is a little better than the fish last night," he said agreeably.

"The fish was terrible. At least this is only burnt on one side."

He took the fork that Gramps handed him and lifted up the meat to see that indeed the side that was down on his plate was only partially burned.

"You're definitely getting better. I think you probably ought to be the full-time chef."

Gramps snorted. "If your grandmother could hear you now," he started.

"She'd agree with me wholeheartedly. She always said you needed to learn."

Gramps snorted again, but he knew he was right. Grandma passed away three months ago, and neither one of them had gotten over her passing yet. In fact, that might have had something to do with the fact that he had gotten suspended for the first month of the season.

He might have been a little sensitive about it at the time, flying off the handle when he shouldn't have.

Unfortunately, he already had the reputation of a hothead, and what he had done had turned out worse than what he had intended.

No one was hurt any more than needing a few stitches, but still. He'd been suspended, and that was that.

Both of them were silent for a bit, and then he said, "Let's pray." Their agreement was whoever cooked, the other person prayed.

Gramps didn't say anything, just bowed his head.

"Lord God, please bless the food and keep it from killing us. Amen." That had been the gist of his prayer for the last week. So far, God had seen fit to answer with a yes.

Not that he was afraid to die, because he wasn't, he just didn't want to if it could be avoided for another half-century or so.

"Amen," Gramps echoed, and without any more conversation, they both dug into their food, knowing that if they didn't eat it, they were going to go to bed hungry.

The chicken was disgusting, dry on the inside and crispy/tough on the outside, but the view of the lake was beautiful, the breeze calming with the way it bent the grasses and rippled the water. It smelled fresh and clean and was just cool enough to be refreshing without being chilling.

Just ten yards or so from their cabin, there was a steep drop of about five feet to the shore. The cabin beside his had a slightly steeper drop, and on down the beach the shore rose up in bluffs that overlooked the lake.

Wesley and Gramps had only been there for five days, and he hadn't made it to the little town that sat at the top of the bluffs, but he figured it was probably a pretty view. He had walked down along the lake to the pebble beach that was right beneath the bluffs, although he hadn't gone the day he had arrived. It sounded like there was some kind of party going on, and he wondered if maybe he had made a bad choice. Perhaps teens hung out here since it was so isolated. Possibly even gangs. Not that he was afraid, he just didn't want to be bothered. He was supposed to be working on his memoir.

He hadn't expected to have someone in the cabin beside his either. When he'd bought it, he hadn't even realized he was going to have a neighbor.

But she—he was pretty sure it was a woman—kept to herself, which was just fine by him.

"Why don't you get over and introduce yourself to the neighbor? Be neighborly. You ought to bake a pie and take it over. That's what your grandma would do."

He was going to say if Gramps baked the pie, he would take it over, but he didn't want to scare the neighbors away.

"I think the definition of being neighborly is to let people know if you like and appreciate them. If I were to bake a pie, they would get the exact wrong impression."

"Maybe I could get on that there computer thing and look up a video. That's what everybody else does."

"Then I would have to go to the store and buy all the ingredients, and that seems like an awful lot of work to put into something that probably isn't going to turn out very well. Plus, I'm supposed to be writing a book. I don't have time to bake pies."

"You have time for what you make time for," Gramps said, and if Wesley had heard that once growing up, he heard it a million times.

His mom hadn't been married when she got pregnant with him, and she dropped her baby off with her parents before she split.

She calmed down from her wild ways and now had a nice family in Tulsa, and now that he was a big superstar hockey player, she wouldn't mind having something to do with him, but she hadn't been interested his entire growing-up years, and he wasn't overly interested now.

"I think I better make time to write a book. If I want to keep playing hockey anyway."

"Is that what you want?" Gramps said, with a change of voice that so often happened with him. He'd be gruff and tough one minute and tender and compassionate the next. Gramps really was a softy on the inside, but his edges were a little bit rough. Wesley could relate.

"Yes," he promised, and then he continued, because it was Gramps.

"I can't imagine my life without hockey. I don't want to imagine my life without hockey," he said, shrugging one shoulder as he stuffed another bite of chicken in his mouth. He hadn't intended to go on a diet and in fact probably shouldn't. He could stand to gain a few pounds after losing weight after his grandma's funeral. She was the one who had always fed them, made sure he was eating okay, and told him about the evils of fast food and take-out.

He smiled thinking about it. She had always cared about them. More than anything else in the world. They were her life.

It was...nice to have someone who truly cared and wanted the best for you, someone that you knew was always going to be on your team. That was Gram. Gramps too, but he was a little rougher about it. And he couldn't cook.

"All right then, I guess you need to write the book, but I'm not going to be the full-time chef. You'd think a fellow would get some sympathy after he loses his wife of sixty-four years, but no, now the kid wants me to cook on top of me dealing with my grief." Gramps used his fork to cut into one of the still-hard beans on his plate. "My dentures are never going to be the same."

"Maybe we could hire a cook."

"And where exactly would they stay?" Gramps asked reasonably.

There were two single beds in the cabin. One on one side of the room, one on the other. There was a bathroom in the back, a fairly large bathroom, which must have been a recent addition, since the siding in the back of the cabin didn't match the rest of it. They'd done it well, with a large tile shower, tile floor, and a double sink. The bathroom was actually his favorite part of the cabin. The rest of it was kind of run down.

Gramps had been a carpenter by trade, but that had been years ago. Wesley had worked for him through high school, in the spring and early summer when he wasn't playing hockey.

Still, he had a book to write first, and any cooking or carpentry had to wait.

"Did I ever mention that I failed composition in high school?"

"I was there, remember? You did take summer school, and I had to take time off work every day to drive you to the school for your classes, then go pick you up and take you back to work with me. Do you think I'd forget something as inconvenient as that?" Gramps gave up on the fork, set it on the banister, and picked the beans up with his fingers. Wesley could hear them crunching on the other side of the porch where he sat.

Or maybe that was just his dentures flapping. He wasn't sure.

"How am I supposed to write a book when I couldn't even pass high school composition?"

"You managed to pass in college."

"That was because I had a girlfriend to write my papers for me." Wesley looked across the porch at Gramps and lifted his shoulder.

"She didn't write them for you; she helped you with them. There is a difference," Gramps said. But he continued to look at Wesley, as though waiting for Wesley to confirm what he'd always said.

"All right. You're right. I couldn't cheat. Because that would have been wrong, but I needed a lot of help, and she wasn't really my girlfriend."

"I know. You were just doing her a favor, increasing her prestige or whatever on campus by supposedly dating the big up-and-coming hockey player, and she returned the favor by helping you with your composition class."

Wesley nodded, wondering how much more of the chicken he could shove down and taking a big swig of his lemon water.

He had actually been the one to proposition the girl. She had thought he was going to do something lascivious and had shut him down right away, and then, when he had gotten to the meat of the issue, she laughed and said that she never thought of doing anything like that, but it might be fun.

She was shy and a little quiet, and by the time they had amicably "broken up," she had ended up being elected their college class president.

He was pretty sure she was having a fairly successful life in state politics, and it wouldn't shock him if she ended up on the national stage at some point. She had been a good girl. Totally refusing to do any kind of cheating, which he'd never asked her to do anyway, but completely willing to tutor him.

And to pretend to be his girlfriend.

He couldn't remember her name off the top of his head, but it had been one of the more fun memories he had of college.

"Maybe the girl over there knows how to cook," Gramps said. "Maybe I could...offer to fix that squeaky screen door of hers in return for a meal."

"Why don't you just leave her alone? She probably wants privacy just as much as we do." And he didn't want to risk her recognizing him or her being interested in some kind of relationship. He didn't have time for either one.

As he was thinking that, a sleek, shiny red sports car motored down the road, pulling in at the cabin beside theirs.

For a moment, Wesley had been afraid he'd been found out, but thankfully whoever was in the car was visiting the neighbors. Unless they had gotten the wrong cottage, which made Wesley want to jump up and run inside. But that would only bring more attention to him, so he sat still, like a rabbit trying not to be seen in the bushes.

"Maybe our neighbor got tired of trying to cook for herself and hired a chef. I wonder if she'd share?" Gramps said, looking curiously at the car as it pulled to a stop.

They waited for a few seconds, and then the driver's door opened. Wesley was almost holding his breath, which was the first time that he realized that perhaps he was a little bit understimulated at the cabin since nothing exciting had happened since they had come, other than the thrice daily burning of a meal. Once, his pork chops had caught on fire and he'd been a little concerned that he might burn the cabin down, but it had quickly been extinguished and was hardly worth mentioning.

A lady, older sixties, early seventies perhaps, stepped out of the car, standing up and looking around, her gaze catching on their porch for just a second before she looked straight ahead at the cottage beside them.

She reached in the car, pulled out a purse, slung it over her shoulder, and then backed up enough to shut the door. She wasn't dressed anything like his grandma, although she must have been about the same age.

"Yeah. I am definitely going to have to make a visit to the neighbor's house now. Can you think of anything else other than the squeaky screen door I could use as an excuse?"

Wesley rolled his eyes. Gramps was just joking. He would never love anyone the way he'd loved Gram, but things had definitely gotten a lot more interesting around here in the last five minutes.

Tap here to see all of Jessie's books!

More books with the characters you love in Raspberry Ridge - read Blueberry Beach and Strawberry Sands!

A Gift from Jessie

View this code through your smart phone camera to be taken to a page where you can download a FREE ebook when you sign up to get updates from Jessie Gussman! Find out why people say, "Jessie's is the only newsletter I open and read" and "You make my day brighter. Love, love, love reading your newsletters. I don't know where you find time to write books. You are so busy living life. A true blessing." and "I know from now on that I can't be drinking my morning coffee while reading your newsletter – I laughed so hard I sprayed it out all over the table!"

Claim your free book from Jessie!